DEL

NORTE

FOREST SERVICE CABIN

COUNTY

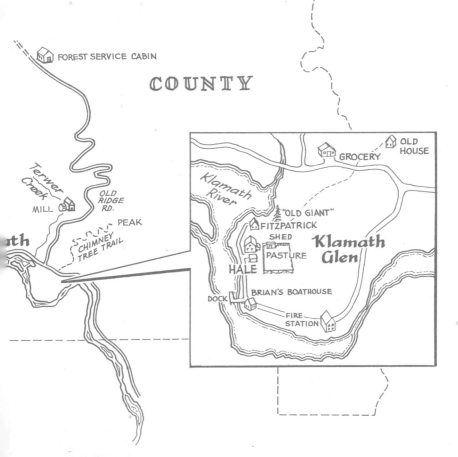

Terwer Creek

MILL

OLD RIDGE RD.

PEAK

CHIMNEY TREE TRAIL

ath

Klamath River

GROCERY

OLD HOUSE

"OLD GIANT"

FITZPATRICK

SHED

PASTURE

Klamath Glen

HALE

DOCK

BRIAN'S BOATHOUSE

FIRE STATION

Beloved
Was Bahamas

*Our warm wishes
to Eric Pfister*

*Harriett E. Weaver
and Bahamas*

BELOVED
WAS
BAHAMAS

A Steer to Remember

HARRIETT E. WEAVER

Author of "Frosty, A Raccoon to Remember"

THE VANGUARD PRESS, INC. NEW YORK

To the wonderful people
of the Klamath River and Crescent City.
Their stamina and inner something during the
Christmas holidays of 1964 could have been
matched only by one very big, very black Angus
steer named Bahamas.

Contents

Contents

ONE

Born to Fame

In California's heavily forested Northwest, which is giant redwood country, a black Angus steer, named Bahamas, has become legend. And he is legend enough to match the mighty trees that witnessed his incredible rise to fame. Partly because of his natural charm, but even more because of what he went through, something special and powerful touched the lives of ten rugged men of forest and sea, a high-school athlete, and a girl. Long will he be remembered, for to know about him is never to forget. This, then, is really Bahamas' story.

Brad Hale, who raised Bahamas, had no warning of all the tumult that lay dead ahead when he dropped off the school bus the Thursday afternoon at the beginning of Christmas recess. At the moment he was concerned only with getting in out of the slicing downpour stinging his face and spattering high off his sou'wester. Like everyone else in redwood country, he was thoroughly sick of the storm. For most of a month now the sky had been dumping itself on the dense big tree forests along the coast. When was it ever going to quit, anyway? With a groan, Brad slung his basketball shoes over one shoulder. Head lowered, hands in pockets, he hunched inside his oilskins and leaned into the fierce wind-driven rain. Then he began to trudge toward the Hale's small ranch at the edge of the cutover area in the curve of the swollen Klamath River.

At the front gate, Brad glanced up and saw his father's red and white pickup in the garage. He reached up under the brim of his sou'wester and brushed aside an unruly lock of blond hair.

"Cripes!" he muttered, his eyes narrowing. "Mill's closing today sure enough. Now what!"

No one had to tell him what. He knew. He wondered if his logger father, Monty Hale, was pacing the living room floor, puffing on his pipe. Brad dreaded going in, for without fail these layoff times had a way of exploding into crises. He was curious about what chain of circumstances this one would set off.

Shaking off his depression, Brad concentrated on walking into the house as if things were about as usual—although he knew they weren't and had a creepy hunch they never would be again.

Monty was touching a match to kindling in the fireplace when Brad entered. Brad glanced at the broad back and powerful shoulders. "Hi, Dad," he called as casually as he could and, removing his streaming sou'wester, sauntered on into the kitchen to say hi to his mother.

Jane Hale, like her son strikingly blond, turned away from her Christmas cooky making. Full of interest in his day, she moved toward him immediately, asking if his feet were wet, whether he was hungry. She smiled, but Brad noticed the heightened color of her cheeks and the worry lines creasing her forehead. He tried not to let her know he saw. Instead, answering her concerns one by one, he carried his slicker to the back screened porch to drip. Then he strolled back into the living room and watched his father heft a huge log and place it on the grate above a row of flames that had begun to lick upward vigorously. Their brightness and popping sparks brought cheer to the dark afternoon. At four o'clock, with rain thundering on the roof and spreading over every inch of windowpane, the fire became instantly the heart of the modest home in Klamath Glen.

Brad sat down before it, removed his boots and socks, and set them to one side to dry. "How long'll you be out, do you suppose?" he asked his father hesitantly.

Klamath Glen knew Monty Hale as ruggedly handsome; a man of few words; honest, stubborn, gruff; a capable bull buck—boss of the woods crew that bucked felled timber into log lengths. Before replying, Monty took a deep breath and ran a hand through his thick brown hair. "Won't be out long probably." After a moment he added, "When it stops raining—if it ever does—we'll skin those big logs out of Elk Creek. Have to shore up the road first."

Brad nodded but felt his stomach tighten. Did his father actually believe his reply had sounded convincing? How could he? Not with the whole Northwest half drowned by record storm fronts roaring in off the Pacific, one after another. Not with every creek and river near flood stage, ready to scour the lowlands. And besides, there were other things.

Brad had heard lumbermen saying it was fortunate they had enough logs stacked in their cold decks so they wouldn't need to cut more trees for a while. The torrential downpour had made a mess of every logging road. Klamath Glen men would be out of work for some time to come, maybe months, Brad thought, frowning. You just never could tell.

At school that morning the scuttlebutt had been that the fellers and buckers and catskinners had already been laid off; that the riggers and loaders would be next. From previous winters Brad knew what this would be like. He swallowed furtively and glanced at his father. Monty had picked up his Crescent City paper, snapped the creases out of it, and settled into his big chair to read.

Brad drew his knees up and wrapped his arms around them. For a time he stared moodily into the fire, wriggling his toes and wishing his father would talk with him more about the goings-on in the woods and at the mill and stuff. Here he was, almost a man himself. Fifteen last month. Big for his age. Time to talk back and forth together, especially on things that mattered—like this layoff, for instance. And like Bahamas.

Never would he forget that morning three years ago when he'd asked his father if he could bring home the newborn Angus calf the dairy had offered him. One they didn't expect to last the day, much less the night. He had wanted it desperately. Its querulous blat had sounded so pitiful—like the bleat of the orphaned fawn he had once found under some bracken. And like the fawn, it had snuggled inside his mackinaw, seeking warmth and comfort.

Another thing he remembered, too: While he had pled so earnestly for the tiny black calf, an amused smile was twisting one corner of his father's mouth. Finally Monty had said, "Barnyard animals eat too much. Why don't you go down to the boat dock and see if you can't tame some of the otters that hang around there. They rummage their own groceries."

Brad had thought of no reply. All he could do was shift from one foot to the other unhappily.

"And what about Mike?" Monty asked.

Brad had no ready answer for this either. What could he say? For a donkey, Mike was a good pal, all right. The best for riding along the river and up and down steep trails. Cussed and independent, though.

"Calf isn't going to make it if I don't take him," Brad had declared. "He has to have special care."

Monty had laughed at that and up had gone his heavy eyebrows. "Oh?" was all that came out of him, Brad recalled. Nothing more. So he had pressed his cause, his voice rising. "Dad, they want to *give* him to me and I know I can save him."

Afterward he had stood there, wondering what better reasons than these there could possibly be for bringing home the calf, and waiting while his father smiled down at him as if all he had said was kind of funny. He would always remember the hopelessness of his cause the morning of the confrontation. Yet, later the same day, unbeknownst to his father, he had eased stealthily through the shed's back door—lugging the little calf.

Recalling how he had succeeded in keeping it made him wince. To rid himself of the memory, Brad jammed his heels against the hearthstones and pushed back from the booming fire. He rubbed his shins gingerly. Already his new jeans were too short for him. He'd have to figure on new ones a size larger.

New ones? He laughed soundlessly. There wouldn't be anything new around this house for some time to come. If this rain kept up much longer, they'd be lucky to have meat on the table. Thank goodness he had saved that twenty Brian Turner had paid him for last month's work at the boathouse, scraping, painting, and repairing. On the Lower Klamath, winter was the season of readying for summer and fall rushes of salmon and steelhead fishermen on the river. It had been providing him not only with spending money but also supplementary food for Mike and Bahamas.

Suddenly the idea occurred to him that he probably could help out with household expenses. He cleared his throat. "Dad?"

Monty looked up from his paper.

Brad tried to sound casual. "I've been thinking. Believe I'll see Brian. I'm pretty sure he'll be able to use me several hours more a week between now and New Year's. Last Saturday we pulled the boathouse back from the bank and Brian says we need to . . ."

Monty's face darkened. His voice grated as he interrupted. "Brad, Brian's been giving you a lot of hours now.

More than he can afford. Put that time on your school-work. Let's see some better grades."

He emphasized his words with a jerk of the paper to turn the page. A moment later he was again engrossed in his reading. Or so it appeared.

Brad frowned. He could understand a man's reluctance to admit needing assistance, but did his father have to blast out like that, even if he were feeling edgy?

Before he could fret further, Monty's voice, deep and resonant and more gentle now, came from behind the newspaper. "Anyway, son, thanks for the offer. If I need your help, I'll say so."

Brad's shoulders sagged. He rose and went to his room to put on some dry socks and boots. He'd go to the shed and be with Bahamas. Out there, at least, he could feel like someone who mattered.

He strode through the kitchen and onto the back porch, where he donned his oilskins thoughtfully.

How well he knew that Monty had always gone all out to keep from centering attention on him or giving in to his every wish. Often through the years he had made speeches about this. "Son," he would warn, "you got three strikes on you, being an only child. Most only-children are spoiled rotten. People can't stand 'em. No one will ever be able to say I did that to you. I'll see to that."

He'd seen to it, all right. Brad couldn't remember ever having been called spoiled by either friends or neighbors. Neither could he remember any of them remarking enviously to him: "You lucky so-and-so. Great to pal around with your dad like you do—backpacking, fishing, riding all the trails in the Six Rivers, raising Bahamas. Man, that's cool, none of our school gang living in the Glen or anything."

Brad yanked tight the chinstrap on his sou'wester and blew out noisily. Why in blazes did Klamath Glen have to be so small and he the *only* teen-aged boy in it!

Okay, so his dad was still trying to save him from the certain tragedy of being spoiled; yet any dad should have known all along that a guy's caring would find its way to somebody or something. And it had . . . it had. Bahamas had been soaking it up like a big black sponge ever since that scary day he was spirited into the shed and hidden in some of Mike's straw. So what, if he *was* only a steer?

Well, things sometimes had fearful and wonderful ways of working out. They took the darndest twists. Brad wondered what the next twist was going to be. Of one thing he felt positive: There would be a next. He could bank on that.

TWO

The Spark

Be out in the shed," Brad called over his shoulder. Then, ducking his head, he leaped into the rain and sloshed up-slope to the closest corner of the seven-acre pasture. As fast as he could, he let himself into the corral, then the shed. Once inside, he pushed the door shut behind him, stomped the mud and water off his boots, and hung up his shiny-wet raingear.

Snapping on the light, he saw only Bahamas, lying peacefully in the straw. Evidently his father had let the restless donkey out. Mike liked to run and rear and buck through the high grasses before seeking shelter under the thick skirts of the young second-growth redwoods at the other end of the pasture. It was his way of rebelling against the endless downpour. If he couldn't do this, he would pace the shed, often sticking his head out the window and braying until he could be heard all over the Glen.

But not Bahamas, thought Brad, standing before him,

feet spread wide, thumbs hooked into his jeans pockets. The old boy just lay quietly, enjoying life without fuss or sweat.

"Hiya, Mophead," Brad joked, grinning wryly. "Glad to see me?"

Bahamas licked out his tongue as if to invite his visitor closer. Brad dropped to his knees, wrapped his arms around the sleek neck, and gave it a bear hug. Then he backed off and sat cross-legged, Indian fashion, where he could run his fingers through the pile of ringlets on the broad forehead. He liked to rumple them so he could watch them spring back into curl. He also liked to have his hands and face sandpapered by the rough tongue.

Brad knew he and his steer were *simpatico*. He could tell by the orange flecks that lighted the steer's eyes whenever they looked at him—orange flecks never dulled by awnings of thick lashes.

And so it had been with the two of them ever since that long-ago morning at the dairy, when Brad had eased into the straw beside the trembling hour-old calf, pulled it into his lap, and buried his cheek in the still-damp coat. How clearly he remembered breathing in the smell of the newly created—a scent free of barn odors, even of hay. There he had remained until nearly noon, cozying the pathetic little thing, wanting it for his own.

Brad was reflecting on this when all at once the shed door opened and, propelled by a gust of wind and rain, his mother burst in.

"Heavens!" she laughed, throwing her weight against the door. "Seems like it's coming down harder all the time."

Brad greeted her with a warm, "Hi, Mom." He had always welcomed his mother out here. To him she was not only good to look at but good company as well. In a way, she made up a bit for the lack of teen-agers in the Glen . . . and for a companionable father. Thanks to her, he didn't miss his school friends, including his new interest, Gildee Griffin, *quite* as much.

Brad watched Jane pull off her streaming raingear, hang it up slowly and carefully, then drop down beside him. He could see that she had something on her mind.

After making herself comfortable, Jane studied her son for a moment, then came directly to the point.

"I just thought you ought to know, Brad, that your father really does appreciate the offer of your hard-earned money."

Brad's eyes fell. There was an awkward pause.

Jane went on: "He understands you better than you imagine. He's well aware that you've had to make all your own fun—fishing, hunting, working for Brian, enjoying your donkey, raising and babying a big steer, being so active in 4-H. He thinks it's great that you haven't let being an only child get you down."

Brad could muster no reply.

When Brad said nothing, his mother spoke more forcefully. "You must realize, Brad, that this layoff at the mill has hit Dad pretty hard. He knows we're facing no work for maybe months . . . and Christmas almost here."

In a softer tone Jane added, "Most certainly he would count on you in an emergency. Someday he'll turn to you for help. He will. You'll see."

Brad, studying his hands, wondered what kind of

disaster it would take to bring this about. Anxious to cover up and change to a more comfortable subject, he forced a laugh and gave Bahamas several resounding slaps on the shoulder.

"Isn't he something, Mom? How'd he ever get so big?"

"And so spoiled?"

They both laughed then. Jane, her eyes suddenly merry, smoothed the collar of her dress. "You mean you've forgotten?" she bantered.

It had long been a joke between them. Every once in a while they went over Bahamas' beginnings, just for the happy remembering: how Brad, not getting an answer from Monty, had wrapped the tiny calf in an old bathrobe and lugged it home from the dairy. Almost in a panic over what he had done without his father's permission, he had slipped into the kitchen and warmed some of the cow's first milk, then hurried back to the shed with it in a baby bottle he had borrowed. Late that evening he had climbed out his bedroom window and tiptoed out to snuggle the little one through the long cold night.

Brad remembered, too, what had taken place the next morning when Monty appeared unexpectedly in the shed and found them—the calf, still alive, frothy milk bubbles dripping from his chin; the mostly empty bottle nearby; Brad covered with straw, down on his hands and knees, ecstatic and shiny-eyed, rolling his forehead against that bunch of curls.

"Boy, was I shook!" Brad said, recalling it for his mother's amusement. "That left eyebrow of Dad's started edging up and I thought sure I was done for." He frowned, reliving the electric instant when, open-mouthed, he stared up at his burly logger father looming above him.

Jane's smile was knowing. "Then?"

"Well, I thought fast, believe me. I said, 'You ought to see this, Dad. He's Bahamas and we're fighting. Watch, now.'" Brad went on to remind his mother of the fight on television the night before, when they had watched the Cuban heavyweight, Bahamas-Somebody-or-other, knock out a Kid Lobo in the very first round.

Jane nodded.

"So all over again I got down on my arms, my behind sticking up in the air, and rolled my forehead against Bahamas' hard little noggin real easy-like, you know. Then I sat up and grinned at Dad and yakked some more, lickety-split, stalling, trying my darndest to figure so he wouldn't make me take my little calf back."

Jane cocked her head. "And you didn't have to."

Brad blew out a breath and flopped backward into the straw. He was silent while his hand groped until it found the great black side, which, in breathing, was slowly rising and falling. He grasped a fistful of the wiry hair.

"No, I didn't have to. All Dad said was: 'Mind you, son, donkeys sometimes kill calves. If Mike don't accept yours, one of them will have to go. One or the other.' He meant it, too."

Brad let out a low whistle. His mother, still smiling, waited.

"Well, good old Mike single-handedly saved the day. Just like in a movie, here he comes, trotting in from pasture right through the corral and up to the window there while Dad was still zeroed in on me. If we'd rehearsed a week, it couldn't have been more perfect."

Grinning broadly, Brad went over for her how the donkey had snuffed noisily and stretched his ungainly head and neck in through the window at the right psychological moment. His eyes had been alert and intent, his ears pertly forward as he studied the tiny bewildered creature lying there in *his* straw. It was giving off strange smells that caused him to wriggle his nostrils and curl his upper lip. For some time he gazed inquisitively at the newcomer, but not once did he snort or paw the ground, although curiosity set him trembling.

Brad laughed. "You know, I think Dad was impressed."

"I know he was," Jane chuckled. "When he came back to the house that morning, he was shaking his head and rumbling in that deep voice of his, 'Bahamas! Of all things—*Bahamas!* That little critter's about as much like that fighter as I am like the King of Siam. With a name like that, he's bound to grow into a whopper, and what's more, live forever. And that's all we need around here— a great big fat Angus!' "

Brad's eyes widened. He wet his lips. "If he'd only said that to me!"

Jane thrust out a hand and tousled her son's hair. "He wouldn't have been Monty Hale if he had."

Then she counseled seriously, "Now that you're older and can understand better, maybe you could do some reaching out. Maybe then he . . ." Jane did not finish. She glanced at her watch, gasped in surprise, and scrambled to her feet. "The meat loaf!" she exclaimed. Quickly donning her raingear, she called good-by and ducked out into the storm.

After she had gone, Brad leaned against Bahamas.

He stretched an arm across the broad back and allowed his fingers to probe the shaggy winter coat, all the while breathing deeply of the earthy smells around him. He could bring to mind so clearly how the shed door had banged after his father that morning; how the noise had startled the calf so much that Brad had gathered it to him, holding it close, rocking back and forth until at last, after a quavering sigh, the trembling had stopped.

All day he had cuddled the little one. Often he looked into the brown eyes that gazed up at him, vaguely at first, then shining with warm lights. No matter how many years he lived, he would always be able to feel the cold wetness of the nose, tucking itself up under his chin, sending shivers of delight racing all over him. Vivid still was the utter delight of it.

Brad grew pensive as his hand smoothed the black vastness that was Bahamas now. He was filled with wonder. How could more than twelve hundred pounds of flesh, bones, and personality grow from anything so small and fragile? It had, though. Perhaps being a bottle baby for so many months wasn't as idiotic as some people in the Glen, including his father, had declared it to be.

But still disturbingly haunting were the crucial hours of that morning long ago when he had watched as life hung suspended between one breath and the next; when he had whispered again and again, "Bahamas! Bahamas!" and with his own boundless vitality tried to fan the tiny spark that, moment by moment, threatened to go out; a spark so feeble it could not even be thought of as a will to live.

More pleasant to remember was the late afternoon

when quite miraculously the spark brightened and flickered into flame. Just before sundown the calf lifted his blocky head, laid it on Brad's shoulder, and wafted warm breath into his ear. From then on, it was plain to see that life would not be denied.

Brad smiled. Bahamas had slipped into the Hale family life as smoothly as a canoe glides across a pond. After he had been catered to and spoiled for a time, his baby shyness had given way to a pixie spirit. As a full-grown steer, he had won the hearts of all the friends and Glen residents who came to visit him until they tended to think of him as a character rather than an animal.

Only a week ago one of the Glen's catskinners had said, in attempting to explain him: "The critter's not one to stomp and snort. Durn fool always looks like some fat kid stuffed to the gills with ice cream. You know—no fight. Happy to eat and be lazy, be lazy and eat. And adore his humans. Yeah, always that."

Brad had to admit this was how it was. Bahamas had become an individual of distinction with an identity all his own.

Years afterwards northcoast residents recounting their favorite legends would tell how he never lost that special identity. Not even during those horrifying hours at Christmastime.

A Christmastime exactly three days away now.

THREE

Bottle Baby

No one expected Christmas to be a merry one with the mills closing, the men out of work, and the rainy season far wetter than usual. Once any redwood country winter sets in, everything soon becomes thoroughly soaked. This year, rain fall was already approaching the hundred-inch mark. And it was still coming down as if it meant to continue until time for the summer fogs to take over, ordinarily by the end of May. The forest had long been green and lush and aromatic from the ground cover of oxalis to the cloud-sweeping treetops.

Dominating this majestic wonderland were giants well over thirty stories high, up to twenty feet through, and a thousand or two years old. The tall Goliaths towered over man and beast and logging trucks as if they were ants in a cornfield.

All six rivers draining the coastal mountains empty into the Pacific. Each is a fisherman's heaven. The largest, the Klamath, rises far inland near Oregon's Crater Lake. From there it descends steeply through a grandly rugged wilderness of peaks and canyons and Indian reservations until, after a number of meandering curves, it empties into the sea.

Two miles above the mouth, at the northern approach to a long, impressive concrete bridge guarded by stone bears, stood the village of Klamath. Four miles above, the river makes a wide glassy loop, mirroring darkly the mountains through which it flows. Within this loop nestles the sports fishing community of Klamath Glen. On the hillside above is the mill; on its upper curve, a trailer park called Frog Pond; on its lower curve, several small homes, among them the Hale place.

The houses had been built near enough to the river so that Brad could, from his front yard, haul in salmon of fifty pounds and more, while below him the deer drank peacefully. On days when the heat drove animals down from the shadeless logged-off patches, he could watch mother bears sitting in the shallows, bathing their cubs.

But there was a price tag on all this. The Hales, along with their close neighbors, the Fitzgeralds and a half dozen others, paid for it every winter in vigilance and uneasiness.

Big storms, moving in off the sea, turned even the tiniest rivulets into raging torrents. The Klamath nearly always ran wild. It came thundering down through roadless gorges of first the Cascade Range and then the Trinity before bursting out into salt water from the broad floodplain of its lower reaches. During such times, the residents of Klamath Glen learned to expect trouble along the banks.

Brad was expecting it now. He knew his father was too. On several occasions he had seen Monty peering out over the river, noting the rise after each freshet, the fall in the respites between. This was just something everyone did. It was an anxious time.

The afternoon after the mill shut down—Friday—the rains suddenly stopped. The heavy clouds rose from the trees and a pale sun came out. Brad felt certain the sky would soon again let loose. Hurriedly he turned Bahamas out to pasture, saddled Mike, and galloped around the far side of their acreage in the direction of the mountain behind the Glen.

Riding along, Brad had to laugh because they were bound for Chimney Tree Trail. It had been Mike's decision. Given his head, he invariably started for one of his favorite spots high above the valley. Up there the only sounds were of wind combing the grasses and the faint boom of the surf in the distance. Just why the donkey was so addicted to the loftiest places he could find was a mystery, even to Brad.

"Mike'd rather snort up a steep trail than mosey along the level any day," Brad had often explained.

"Like along the river?" someone would question.

"Yeah, like along the river, doggone it. I'd like to keep track of the salmon resting in the deeper eddies. Besides, that'd give me more time to watch the otters bellying down their mudslides into the water. But I have to humor Mike a bit, you know, and with him it's mountaintops."

So up they'd climb to Eagle View or Buzzard's Rest or Chimney Tree Peak, their present goal.

On their way to any of these points they'd pass through at least one dimly lighted grove of redwood giants, already vast and gnarled with age when Columbus set out for the New World. Often they plodded streamside up some dank canyon whose steep-sided walls dripped with maidenhair and five-fingered ferns, sparkling with dew. Sometimes, on another trail, they lost themselves among woodwardia ferns and tiger lilies taller than a teen-ager on horseback.

After the fog burned off, everything glistened in the light. Young redwoods, their branches tipped with the bright green of new spring growth, looked as if they had been touched up by some unseen brush. The wide leaves of the madrones shone with the luster of things individually washed and waxed. Gradually the blue of the sea deepened until it glittered with billions upon billions of salty diamonds.

And the smells! Depending upon where and in what season Brad was riding, he could breathe the delicate fragrance of creamy azaleas that splashed the somber green of the dense forest; or he could sniff the spicy aromas the open hillside herbs loosed as they soaked up the warming sun.

These things stirred Brad. He supposed that all the beauty maybe did prove there actually was a God—like Gildee had insisted that day last summer while they were hiking up to Silver Falls. God must be everywhere, she had said. All around them all the time. So how could anyone ever be lonely or in danger?

After much thought on this brand new idea, Brad conceded that Gildee just could be right. Out in the wilds alone with Mike he might admit such a notion. But speak of this before anyone else? Never. He'd keep strictly to earthly fact when describing his rides into the back country.

For such adventuring, Brad couldn't think of a finer buddy than Mike. In telling him so now, Brad reached down and thumped a shoulder companionably.

The donkey's gallop slowed to a walk. They were rounding the huge surface roots of the Old Giant, a redwood so mighty that early-day loggers decided to leave it standing when they clearcut the Glen. A few minutes later, Brad and Mike approached a cluster of structures not far above the foot of Chimney Tree Trail. It was an assortment of barns and sheds of various sizes and shapes. All were connected and led roof by roof from alongside the trail to the eaves of a two-story old-fashioned white house with an upstairs-view window and gingerbread trim here and there. On the tip of the one turret was a red weathervane. The old house had stood vacant for many years.

When Brad and Mike came to it they were forced to stop. During the night a slide had rolled across the trail and onto the lowest of the roofs.

The donkey side-stepped and blew out noisily. Then he planted his feet as wide apart as he could and stretched his head and neck forward. Aquiver, he eyed the whole thing.

Suddenly Brad realized that Mike was not so much wary as fascinated by the stair-step roofs leading up to the main one and now, thanks to the slide, all within easy reach. To him they represented a challenge.

Brad reined in. "Here! Here, Mike!" he barked. "You can't." He glanced at the sky. "Let's get home fast."

As they came galloping along the path under the spreading pepperwoods and maples in the Hale back yard and jogged into the corral, Brad saw Bahamas at the other end of the pasture. He had backed up to the biggest redwood stump and was busily rubbing his rump back and forth across the only place on it not overgrown with prickly wood rose bushes. His face reflected the pure bliss that filled him.

"Leave it to you to choose the prettiest spot in the pasture for scratching yourself," Brad said aloud. "Leastways it was until the rain pounded the blooms all off."

He threw back his head and laughed. Wildflowers seemed to have a strange fascination for Bahamas. The steer had always passed up thick grass to go and stand or lie in a patch of lupine or mountain iris or Indian paintbrush. One way or another he'd find his way to flowers or they to him—as, for instance, by those simpering ten-year-old Mackey twins up the road.

Brad grimaced. It wasn't that he didn't like girls. That would be the day! But these two impossibly silly ones had gone too far last spring, fixing that garland of dogwood and rhododendron blossoms and hanging it around Bahamas' neck. So what if it had made him look and smell sweet, as the girls had shrilled so triumphantly. For a sleek, fully grown Angus to be decked out in this manner was degrading and dumb stupid.

That evening, pitching alfalfa into the manger, Brad

had vowed to forestall further indignities. He'd laid the law down firmly, emphasizing his words with every forkful. First of all, there would be no more bottle, which there wasn't; and Bahamas would have to start acting his age, which he didn't.

Never before had Bahamas heard such a harsh tone coming from anyone, much less Brad. Startled, he stopped chewing momentarily. With wisps of hay dangling loosely from the hairs of his chin, he regarded the other with mild curiosity. Then peacefully, as he did everything, he lowered his thick lashes and set his jaws in motion again, slowly, meditatively.

Brad might have eliminated the bottle months before had he known what some of the Glen residents were saying.

Those who knew him readily agreed he had done quite a thing, all right, in saving and raising the Angus. But to what end? they asked. Just to keep for a pet? Just to cater to? Most meat animals at a certain age and weight . . .

Others of Bahamas' friends and neighbors merely smiled and admitted he had such an enchanting way of making one feel appreciated that going over to the Hale place to give him his bottle now and then was real amusing.

A few howled with laughter. A big steer still on the bottle? What they meant, of course, was that other young things around there graduated from infancy after a reasonable length of time. But not Bahamas. For a huge black Angus to create the image of a wistful spirit, delicate and undernourished, was no small feat, but Bahamas managed it neatly. And so he continued to be a conversation piece in Klamath Glen.

As he reached twelve, then eighteen months, and five hundred, then nine hundred pounds, visitors found the problem of hanging onto one end of a calf bottle while he pulled at the other not so much a privilege as an athletic event. Consequently, with his steady increase in heft, there were dropouts among his less muscular callers.

Those who did come Bahamas received happily, accepting carrots, pats, and hugs from most, sly ridicule from several, and, not knowing which was which, loving them all; dragging his rough tongue over faces and necks, sucking any fingers and dresses he could get hold of, blowing little breathes of delight on every extended hand. For everyone alike he radiated affection. And the passing years had not diminished his ardor one bit.

Turning Mike loose that gloomy December day, Brad sauntered through the wet grasses of the pasture to his steer and was overwhelmed with the customary welcome. The rough tongue rolled out and curled over his cheek, scrubbing it until he ducked away.

"Baby, you're the limit!" Brad protested mildly. "Why don't you tear around and paw the ground like other black Angus around here? Why can't you show some kind of steam?"

Bahamas responded in the usual way. He flapped his ears at a passing gnat. Then he gazed soulfully at Brad, mooed softly, and nosed the boy's knit cap off his head. He always did this if he could. Well, not always, Brad reminded himself—there was the matter of the straw hat.

During one of the afternoons when Mike and Bahamas had romped in the pasture, chasing each other round and round and finally teaming up for pranks, the donkey had snatched the hat off his head and made off with it. With Bahamas joyfully running interference for him, Mike had been able to retain possession for the better part of an hour. Despite Brad's basketball experience, he could never get close enough to even make a grab for it. In the end, the two animals, tiring of their game, had shared the thing, eating it with apparent relish.

Chuckling about this, Brad bent over to retrieve his cap.

Before his fingers could touch it, he was suddenly pitched forward. He hit the sodden earth with grunt and thud. Every now and then he forgot and stooped for something in front of Bahamas, only to be bunted squarely amidships.

While picking himself up and wiping the wet grass and clover off his face, Brad heard feminine laughter, not all of it his mother's. He spun around to see Gildee standing beside her. Both were leaning on the pasture fence watching him.

FOUR

Gildee

Hi, there!" his visitor called. "Mom and Dad had to come down and check on Grandma. They dropped me off."

Brad sauntered toward the fence, appraising Gildee as he went, noticing how the jaunty rainhat set off the ringlets of red hair that framed her face. She was almost as tiny as his mother, and like her, not pretty but interesting; and the same day in and day out—always gusty and friendly.

As he approached, Gildee called out again. "I told you someday I'd be down to take a look at that famous steer of yours. I don't have but a few minutes. The folks'll want to get back to town fast. The road is a string of slides and slipouts all the way from Crescent City. And it's going to get worse any minute they say."

"Glad you came, Gil," Brad said somewhat awkwardly. "You met my mom?"

"Oh, we're already good friends," Jane put in.

"We've been watching Bahamas keep you in line," Gildee said, a laugh in her voice.

Brad grinned.

Gildee's eyes fairly danced as they gazed past him. "So that's your Bahamas," she cried. "Isn't he a whopper!"

"That's because he was a bottle baby until he was eighteen months old," Jane said.

"Mom!"

"Well, he was—and so what? He liked his bottle and you liked giving it to him every night. And you can't say he didn't thrive on it."

Gildee rolled her eyes. "Did he ever."

Brad had to smile in spite of himself. This was what happened every time. People would look at his big Angus and exclaim simply, "Wow!" and there never could be any question as to what they meant.

Mike could open wide his homely jaws and bray his version of grand opera all he wanted, but the attention would still be on Bahamas. Even when Mike came tearing across the pasture, as he was doing this minute, upending himself like an outboard in a choppy sea, Bahamas, without moving a muscle, would somehow remain the center of interest.

Gildee laughed as she watched the donkey rush up alongside Bahamas and nip him, starting a chase.

For some time the two charged and dodged each other. They faked one direction, swerved and veered off in another. Puffing and blowing, they disappeared behind one of the biggest redwood stumps in the pasture, Bahamas' slender legs carrying his Angus heft with amazing agility and grace.

"Have they always played like this?" Gildee asked.

Brad nodded. "Ever since Bahamas' legs would hold him up—about a week after I got him. From then on, old fire-breathing Mike was the perfect calf-sitter. He'd eat with Bahamas and snuggle close to him every night to keep him warm. And one day, Gil, when the shed door blew shut and separated them, he backed up to it and let fly with his hoofs. Splintered the thing clean to smithereens. I had to go to work and build another'n."

"Twenty-four hours a day Mike watched over Bahamas," Jane said softly. "They grew very attached to each other."

Brad remembered that Bahamas' eyes had brightened with affection for the ungainly giant towering over him, prodding him roughly one minute, scrubbing his face gently the next.

But on more than one occasion he had loved the donkey too much. Had Mike not sensed that Bahamas was young, he might have kicked him whenever the calf's mouth searched yearningly over his warm belly. As it was, apparently mortified beyond all endurance, Mike would flatten his ears to his neck and look behind him as if he feared someone might have witnessed his shame—then trot away indignantly, his head in the air.

Gildee laughed heartily when Brad told her how Mike had finally led Bahamas out of the corral and into the pasture, where he showed him how to kick his heels and scamper around. "When they got tired, old Mike just nudged Bahamas from behind, enough, you know, to throw him down into the grass. He did that lots of times. Sometimes he'd dump him into one of those patches of wild daffodils that pop up out here in our pasture every March or April," Brad explained.

"What then?"

"Nothing. They'd just lie there. Bahamas would stretch out in the warm sun and grasses and wildflowers. Mike would lie down near him, and they'd drowse all afternoon. They still do. Every sunny day they do."

Leaning comfortably on the fence, the three watched Mike tire of play and trot into the shed. Bahamas, left to his own devices, looked around for the first time and noticed his audience. Promptly he began to amble toward them.

As he neared, Brad opened the gate and motioned to his guest. "Come on in and pet him, Gil," he suggested.

The girl hesitated. She glanced questioningly at Jane, who nodded encouragement.

"Don't be afraid. He adores anyone who will pay even the slightest attention to him."

Still unsure of how the huge black steer would accept her, a total stranger, Gildee approached with caution, laid a hand tentatively on his curly bangs, and patted a couple of times. Her voice was mellow when she spoke to him, as if he were still a calf. "What long lashes you have. And what eyes!"

A slow smile spread over Brad's face. He slid his hands into his back pockets and wondered how Bahamas did it. How did he always manage to drag baby talk out of women and girls anyhow?

After a slight pause, Gildee resumed a more matter-of-fact tone. Inclining her head toward Brad, she said, "How come he was on the bottle so long?"

Brad looked away and shrugged. His face colored, but he managed to maintain his customary nonchalance. "He just liked it," he said finally.

He knew, of course, that with Bahamas it was the idea of feeling cozy and cared for like any young thing while he sucked and slobbered and acted as if he were starving, which he wasn't. Besides, it had been his belief that all the fancy calf pails and starters and supplements prescribed for developing sturdy animals was one thing; the hand-held nursing bottle and the gentling that went with it was quite another, and more important by far.

Once more Gildee spoke to Bahamas. "Didn't anyone buy you a nipple pail?" she queried with mock pity.

Brad drew a quick breath and exploded into laughter. "Oh, he had that, all right. He had everything—nipple pail, Calf Mana, alfalfa hay—well, everything. You name it, he had it. The whole bit."

"But most of all, devotion," Jane said. "That's what saved Bahamas." She paused, trying to find the right words. "I guess you could say that anything so loved as he was—and is—simply could not die."

Gildee nodded, her eyes suddenly serious.

All at once, and with no warning whatever, dark menacing clouds slammed their murky doors on the sun. In less than a minute the sky turned a fluid blue-black. The big front was here.

FIVE

Just
So Much
Beef

Gildee cast a startled glance at the sky. "Look at that!" she exclaimed. "Now we *are* in for it!" Giving Bahamas a hug, she turned to leave. "We'd better hurry before . . ."

She got no farther. Suddenly she was boosted forward, her rainhat falling askew, her arms flailing wildly. Blank surprise flooded her face as she pushed her hat back in place, then faced Bahamas incredulously. When she saw that he had just bestowed his unqualified affection on her, gusty laughter burst from her throat. "Did I ever ask for that!" she gasped.

Jokingly she brushed aside the apologies of Brad and his mother. "It's all right," she said, patting Bahamas' sleek neck, then backing away. "You've given me something real solid to remember you by, my friend, and remember I will. Next time I see you, I'll leave your presence *in reverse only.*"

Once again torrential downpour pounded redwood country.

Gildee called her good-byes and Merry Christmas wishes on the run, for her parents' car already waited at the front gate. Through the rain-spattered window she tossed a wave in response to the two who were waving from the Hale front porch. Then the car pulled away swiftly and headed toward Klamath and the Redwood Highway.

When Brad and his mother walked into their living room, Monty was standing at the window, looking out. "Who was that?" he asked, indicating the car splashing down the road. "Fine-looking girl."

"No one in particular," Brad answered lightly. "Just a girl I go to school with. To see Bahamas."

"I noticed he put his stamp of approval on her. Playing kind of rough, wouldn't you say?"

"She was a good sport about it."

"You didn't tell her you were going to put up a tree out in the shed for Mike and Bahamas again this year, did you?" Monty asked. He was hoping that Brad meant to abandon such kid stuff now that he was in high school. After all, Bahamas was no longer a calf and Brad a mere youngster.

Slowly and deliberately Brad slid his hands into his back pockets. He lifted his chin and held the other's gaze.

"A Christmas tree for the shed? Well—yes, I did tell Gil last week that I was figuring on one. Just like always. A small one."

Monty's reply came out ahead of his thoughts. "Oh? I had an idea maybe you'd outgrown all that."

The instant he spoke, he regretted it. To cover up the

best he could, Monty shrugged his big shoulders and
raked a hand through his hair. He wished he knew how
to deal with teen-agers—or kids of any age. Most especially with the only one he had.

Brad did not respond to his father's remark. Instead,
he walked slowly toward his room, hands still in his
pockets.

Monty stared after him unhappily. "I'm afraid trees are
about all the Christmas any of us is going to have this
year, son," he offered hastily, softening his tone. He didn't
add the rest of what he had been thinking over that day.
This wasn't the time. He'd put it off. Maybe something
would happen so he'd never have to say it.

Brad hesitated in the doorway. "No word from the
mill today?"

"No, nothing, I'm afraid."

"And the weather forecast?"

Monty shook his head. "Radio says the big front is
coming in. Looks like it's already hitting us," he mumbled
wearily. He could not bring himself to mention everything else that was about to hit them too: living expenses
piling up day after day, payments due Monday on their
camper, a dental bill, an insurance policy. . . . Monday.
Only three days from now! Everyone in the Glen who
earned his livelihood at the mill was of course heading
into the same kind of crisis. Monty was mindful that
Brad knew all of this.

The big logger compressed his lips. He had always
worked hard to give his family more than just their daily
needs. There had been several bad times over the years,
but never before had he been utterly cornered with no

choice of how to solve a problem. Never. Not until now. Frowning darkly, he dropped into his easy chair and switched on the transistor radio.

After a few moments he heard Brad call to him just loudly enough to be heard above the announcer: "Dad."

Monty looked around in surprise. He thought the boy had gone out.

Brad's tone was level but earnest. "Dad, don't forget what I said. If I can help—like asking Brian . . . or . . . or anything. . . ."

Monty found he couldn't put together an answer. What he would have to say would not come, not yet anyway. He nodded and turned back to the broadcast, lest his frown be misunderstood. Lest also his eyes betray the misery welling up inside him. Brad must not ask Brian for any more work. The fishing guide had been providing more work than he could really afford. No. There was probably only one way out of their dilemma. *Only one way,* blast it!

As if to himself, Brad said, "Well, I guess I'll go and cut me a small fir before the rain gets any worse. Then I'll trim it." He strode toward the back porch to put on his raingear.

Nestled deep in the redwood forest, Klamath Glen had an abundance of Christmas trees of many kinds and sizes growing all around it. From a window, Monty watched Brad slosh up the nearest hillside, ax in hand, rain thudding off his sou'wester. After the boy had disappeared from view, he again sought his easy chair and sprawled there beside the radio to wrestle further with himself. In his heart was an ache almost too overpowering to bear. What was more, he felt exhausted, beaten.

All at once he awoke to the fact that although the announcer had been talking for nearly an hour, he hadn't heard a word the man had said. He straightened in disgust and flipped off the switch.

In the silence that followed, he got up and, staring moodily into space, wandered into the kitchen. He did not notice Jane busily kneading some bread dough. Without a word he sat down at the table, pulled his pipe from a shirt pocket, and lit it.

For a time Monty smoked in silence. When at last he took the pipe from his mouth and blew a long stream of smoke, he had the unmistakable look of a person who had reached a moment of fearful decision.

Jane gave her dough a final pat and covered it with a damp towel. Then quickly she washed her hands, slid into the chair opposite Monty, and folded her arms on the table.

Glancing up, Monty tried to force a smile. "I guess it's time to start figuring."

Jane encouraged him with her eyes.

Still he held back, fingering the pipe bowl, reluctant to voice what was in his mind. When he did speak at last, it was as if he were shouldering a heavier load than he could carry.

"Looks like a long wet spell ahead," he said, unwilling to meet the subject head on. "We're in for the worst yet. Right now."

"Yes."

"Hard telling when I'll get a call from the mill again. Not for weeks, maybe months, that's for sure."

Jane nodded. "Any other work to be had?"

"None. Don't think I haven't tried." His dark eyes were intense. "Two weeks ago I had this hunch we'd have to close down, so I started asking around. I've canvassed the whole countryside for any kind of job. Any kind."

"I know."

Monty put the pipe back in his mouth, struck a match on his boot sole, and worked overly long at relighting. He knew he was stalling. Before he could blow the match out it had burned his thumb, causing him to jump and snap his fingers. Yet it crystallized his thoughts into words.

"We're in a pretty bad spot just now. For one thing, there's that two hundred dollars worth of insurance premiums to meet next week. We don't dare let them lapse, no matter what. You know what all else there is. Somewhere, somehow, pronto, too, I've got to find some money to tide us over."

Jane studied him for a moment. "Want to tell me about it?" she queried gently.

The big logger did not reply immediately. He got up and strolled to the kitchen window. For a few minutes he stood there, puffing on his pipe, frowning at the fast-darkening afternoon; gazing out at the downpour pounding away on the dreary landscape. Smoke from neighborhood chimneys was rising straight up and flattening out, he noted.

Well, all right, it was. It was. What of it! Monty forced

his attention back to the matter at hand. Face up, Hale, he told himself savagely.

He came out with it now, making a determined effort to keep the timbre of his voice low and calm. Even so, it sounded to him like the voice of doom. "I was thinking," he said, "of Bahamas."

Jane threw him a startled look. "Bahamas? You don't mean you want . . ."

The muscles in Monty's jaw tensed. "I—I have to mean it, Jane. He weighs close to three quarters of a ton. Surely I don't have to tell you what this would mean in dollars and cents."

"But we can't sell Bahamas, Monty!" Jane burst out. "He's one of the family. He's Brad's pet. Brad thinks more of Bahamas than he ever has of anything else. We can't . . ." Her voice trailed off.

With work-calloused hands Monty gestured the helplessness he felt. "I know," he said. "This isn't anything I want or can help. What else is there to do?"

"We can't make beef out of Bahamas, Monty." Jane rose to her feet, her eyes wide and earnest. "We simply can't."

Monty turned toward her defensively, frustration sweeping through him like a summer fire flashing across a tinder-dry hillside.

He lashed out angrily. "Don't make me feel like an executioner, Jane. Be realistic. We can't keep Bahamas forever. You just don't keep great big fat steers 'til they die of old age or something. You sell them for beef. That's what steers are for after a while. That's life."

"I guess it depends on whose life you mean," Jane retorted drily. Her eyes had become bright with mounting anger. She began to clean up the kitchen with quick, jerky movements.

For some time there was silence. Monty puffed furiously on his pipe and fought to get hold of himself. Moments passed before he was able to speak more calmly.

"We shouldn't have let Brad keep Bahamas in the first place. Calves have a way of growing into big animals, particularly the Angus. We were crazy—real crazy."

"No, we weren't," Jane contradicted stoutly. "Brad's taken good care of Bahamas. In the doing, he's learned to raise beef cattle."

Monty gave a short laugh. "Oh, no. He's learned how to raise fat steer babies—not beef."

Breathing hard, Jane shook her head and pushed boldly on.

"Listen, Monty. Because of Bahamas, Brad has decided to be a cattleman. He's doing well in both 4-H and Future Farmers. Most boys his age don't have any objective in view at all."

Monty was not to be talked down. He came back at his wife sharply. "Jane, cattlemen don't keep their animals for pets and feed them on a calf bottle until they're the laugh of the community. When the beasts get just so big, they're sold. For beef. *Beef!* The rancher tries to make a profit on each one so he can buy more animals to sell for more profit. It's a business, you know. A *business!*"

Jane, her voice muted, broke in with what her husband had always called "typical feminine reasoning."

"But Bahamas is different, Monty," she appealed. "We

can't sell him. It would break Brad's heart. And don't call Bahamas a . . . a beast! He isn't any old animal. He's . . . well, he's . . ."

"He's our baby," Monty snapped. He could feel his face flushing. "Let's own up to it—that's what you and Brad call him, isn't it? Baby?"

Jane, too, had become thoroughly angry. Eyes glistening, her voice rising, she proceeded to speak her mind.

"I suppose so, if you put it that way. Occasionally we do call him Baby. But what you don't seem to understand is that Bahamas isn't just beef. He . . . he's a person. Selling him would be like selling . . . well, like selling *you*."

For an instant Monty was so taken aback that no retort would come. All he could do was snatch the pipe from his mouth and glare until, at last, an exclamation burst from his throat.

"Honestly, Jane!" he blurted. And since he could muster no further reply, he stalked to the window and stood there, speechless, arms folded tightly across his chest.

Presently, after calming down somewhat, he discovered he had been staring blankly through the shed window. By the electric light there he could see Brad moving about.

Monty's thoughts raced on. The kid was devoted to his two animals, no question about that. Much of his spare time was spent in currying and brushing and feeding them or cleaning their quarters and putting down fresh straw. Always something, even if it was only patting and talking to them—especially Bahamas. Yes, drat it, *especially* Bahamas, Monty thought bitterly.

Jane sauntered back to her husband and slipped an arm

around his waist. Together they stood looking at the rain bouncing off the shed roof.

Monty knew, and he felt sure Jane knew, that inside the shed Brad was following the pattern of the two previous Christmases. He had cut a fir, fixed it in a bucket, and set it on the rough-hewn table in the far corner beside the manger. From its boughs he had hung icicles and red balls and tinsel. Monty was also sure the boy had already placed on the very tip the tiny angel with the filmy wings and outstretched arms. At that moment he was probably standing between Mike and Bahamas, an arm over each, while they gazed at the new brightness in the shed. No doubt Brad was laughing at the way they were viewing it. He had always believed they saw themselves in the shiny red balls. Monty supposed that Christmas morning they would receive their share of attention and whatever goodies the family might have. Brad would see to that.

Months afterward, Monty remembered mulling over all of these things as he and Jane had stood at the window, looking out into the shed. But how he wished he had known then that, come Christmas, neither Mike nor Bahamas would enjoy their holiday treats!

SIX

How
to Help

The day grew dark and dismal. The rain settled down to a steady hum. Jane and Monty watched it, saying nothing, lost in thought.

Jane was first to break the silence. "You know, Monty," she mused, "we must find a way."

Monty made no response.

Jane glanced at him cautiously. "We simply can't expect Brad to give up his steer, even to save an insurance policy, as important as it is. Besides," here she paused and visibly braced herself, "besides, I think Bahamas has earned the right to live." She said it quietly.

The effect was anything but that. Renewed frustration surged up in Monty. He strode to the other side of the kitchen, his eyes blazing. "You're just being sentimental now. You can't eat sentiment, Jane, for Pete's sakes. You don't raise steers to be village characters. You raise them to eat!"

"Not Bahamas," was the cool, undaunted reply.

Monty pressed his lips together and stalked out into the back porch, where he put on his oilskins and hard hat and set out through the rain for the corral. Behind him the screened door slammed.

Head lowered, Monty tramped upslope, fuming as he went. Blast this business of Bahamas! He didn't want to sell the Angus any more than Jane did. But now it was a case of "have to." Just as simple as that. They'd have to—and regardless of Bahamas' big brown eyes and a heart full of love for everyone. Didn't Jane know that if there had been any other way he would have taken it? What sort of monster did she think he was anyhow?

After unlatching the gate and splashing angrily through the corral mud, Monty pushed the shed door open a crack. Inside, he could see his son busily grooming Bahamas. The boy always kept his steer as if he were preparing him to step out and lead a parade, Monty conceded, hunching his shoulders against the storm. How was Brad ever going to be told how desperately they needed the money the animal would bring? The big logger clenched his fists. Then he took a deep breath and slipped quickly into the shed's dim interior.

Surprise flashed across Brad's face as he looked up and saw his father. "Well—hi, Dad," he said, and smiled dubiously.

The greeting stopped Monty. He stood motionless and tense, trying to analyze what Brad was thinking. He was sure he could read what was running through Brad's mind. To him it was as loud and clear as if the boy had shouted it. A chill came over him. With an effort he got hold of himself.

"Nice tree," he said, inclining his head toward the brightly decorated fir in the corner.

When Brad's thin smile spread, Monty relaxed somewhat.

"Cut it from the slope the other side of the Old Giant," Brad explained. "Not tall, but full. Does fine. Leastwise, they like it." He indicated with his eyes the two animals. "It sort of includes them in Christmas."

Monty nodded—and debated what to say next.

Much to his relief Brad went on. "I want to get Bahamas brushed down. Mike too." Deftly he shifted the brush to the other hand and gave the steer an affectionate pat.

"Yeah, good idea," Monty agreed, and tried his best to smile. But he was painfully aware that his effort contributed little to the warmth inside the shed. He was glad when all at once the donkey decided to lie down in the straw to sleep away the rest of the afternoon. It provided him with something to say.

"Bet Mike's not going to care much about the brushing," he observed, making an attempt to joke.

Brad laughed guardedly. "Looks that way."

Monty had run out of small talk.

Brad went on working. Bahamas stood quietly and peacefully. Because bliss filled him, he kept grunting small ecstatic murmurs.

Presently Monty cleared his throat, opened his mouth to say something, and closed it again. For want of anything better to do, he studied his hands and saw that they were sweaty. He took off his hard hat and ran them through his hair several times. Glumly he watched Brad work; watched the steer swipe his tongue over the boy's hand; watched as every now and then the Angus received in return a pat or a word of affection—for which he then licked Brad again in a never-ending chain reaction.

With a growing sense of distress, Monty pondered Brad's obvious contentment whenever he was tending Bahamas or riding Mike. He found it easy to conclude, as he had many other times, that although his son had taken part in his share of pranks, he'd never been in any really serious jams. The boy was a decent sort; one to be proud of. Now how was he, Monty, ever going to tell him he would have to give up his steer! Or could he tell him after all?

Plagued with indecision, unsure of how to approach the subject, Monty did not remove his oilskins or even unbuckle them. Maybe he would want to leave without . . . without . . . He rubbed his jaw tentatively and wrestled with his conflicts. If he could just find *some other way*!

In sudden resolve, Monty straightened. Pushing away from the wall against which he had been leaning, he sauntered over to Bahamas and thumped the fat rump with a woodsman's natural vigor. Evidently it was much more vigor than Bahamas was used to from him. The steer swung his head around and rolled his eyes at Monty in wonder and with sound effects. His full-throated bawl revealed only too eloquently how puzzled he was at the unaccustomed attention.

To conceal his embarrassment, Monty coughed. This bought him another minute in which to brace himself before going ahead with his . . . his mission.

He tried to speak lightly. "You've done a good job with Bahamas, son," he ventured after a compelling silence.

Brad looked up. When his gaze met that of his father's over Bahamas' broad back, the pleasure he felt showed in his eyes. He brushed back the stubborn shock of hair and grinned.

Monty knew he had never been exactly lavish with his compliments. Seeing Brad's face, he wished now he had.

"Thanks, Dad."

Monty nodded, stalling. Finally he asked in a low voice, "Have any plans for him?"

Brad stared blankly. He stood back and rubbed the brush bristles absently against the palm of one hand. "Plans?"

"Yes, you know—plans. A fellow always has some goal in mind when he . . . when he takes a calf."

Brad frowned and guided the brush slowly down Bahamas' flank.

Monty could tell he hadn't made himself understood; that Brad was trying to fathom what he was driving at with his double talk; how, therefore, to answer him.

Monty pushed on, intent on finishing what he had started. "He's a lot of beef. You've done well with him."

Monty had emphasized the word "beef" but he didn't think Brad noticed. He did see, though, that the boy was listening. There was an uneasiness about him in the way he glanced up once, then went on brushing deliberately, carefully.

Gathering a small measure of confidence, Monty now asked far too casually, "What do you . . . ah . . . aim to *do* with him?"

That instant, and with a sharp pang of regret, Monty realized he had struck home. Brad caught his breath and looked up quickly, his eyes keen this time.

As he studied his father, the blood began to drain from his face. Wordlessly, he stood without moving. The big logger could almost feel the clammy fingers of dread tightening around Brad's throat, for they were also closing around his own.

Monty hoped Brad would not see how unnerved he was. He swallowed cautiously. At the same time, to ease his growing tension, he moved alongside Bahamas and ran a hand along the great black side. Then he stopped and, taking a deep breath to carry him forward, forced himself to meet Brad's gaze. Doggedly he held it. This was the moment. There was no turning back now. He was committed.

At last his plea came out as kindly as he could say it.

"Son, you wanted to know if you could help out. Maybe . . . maybe you can if you . . . if you will."

"How do you mean?" The question was almost inaudible. But in it Monty detected fear so stark that he had to look away.

"If we could sell Bahamas, I'm pretty sure—I'm almost certain—we would be offered twenty-six cents a pound for him. That's pretty good, you know. And since he weighs . . ."

In a lifeless, quavering voice, Brad broke in. "How do you know we'd be offered that much, Dad?"

Monty shifted uneasily. Intent on hiding his feelings, he walked to Bahamas' head and slid a hand appreciatively down the sleek neck. "I've asked," he said. He felt as if he had passed sentence.

"You've already asked?" Disbelief flooded the handsome face.

After a minute: "Yes, I asked Mr. Everett. You know, Mr. Everett, the Crescent City cattle buyer."

Brad sounded dazed. "And?"

"Well, he thought probably it would depend on . . . on a number of things, of course." Monty was having trouble meeting the stricken look in Brad's eyes. He knew he had dealt the boy the deadliest blow of his life. He wished with all his heart that he could call it back; that Jane had prevented him from ever leaving the house. Too late now.

See this thing through, he told himself grimly. Everyone's had to make bitter decisions sometime in his life. Maybe this was the time for Brad to grow up a little; the time for him to learn to tackle problems head on and be a man about it. Anyhow, hadn't the boy not once but twice volunteered to help, however he could?

Suddenly Monty became aware that Bahamas was going over his hand with that sandpaper-rough tongue of his, tenderly and lovingly—perhaps because, as Brad had insisted to him and Jane many times, the three of them were Bahamas' family. And it did seem that upon them he bestowed his fondest caresses.

The logger was jolted. In a welter of torment, and before he could calculate the effect of such a move on his son, Monty had jerked his hand away. Then, dismayed because he was sure the act had been misunderstood, he scowled and hurriedly put on his hat.

"Shall we . . . shall we think it over, son?" he suggested with a businesslike crispness he did not feel.

There was no response.

Fumbling with the chinstrap of his hard hat, Monty added, "Mr. Everett said he'd come over sometime tomorrow morning to take a look and . . . and to . . . to make an offer."

As if the boy had agreed to a small matter that had been a mere technicality all the time, Monty gave Bahamas a perfunctory slap, opened the door, and stumbled out into the rain.

He did not go immediately to the house. Rather, with face upturned, he strode briskly down the road. The downpour slashed his flesh with bruising force, but he did not notice. He was far too tormented to be conscious of anything except a need to be battered by a power greater than his own.

Inside the shed, Brad stared after his father, his eyes wide with panic, his breath coming in quick shallow gasps. His hands slackened and dropped to his sides. He fell forward against the solid mass of warmth that was Bahamas.

Minutes passed. The ominous roll of rain on the roof swelled to a deafening crescendo.

All at once and with a sharp cry of anguish, Brad flung himself face down in the straw and pounded his fists into it one time after another.

SEVEN

Zero Hour

The day droned on. Mechanically now, Brad went about his chores. He felt numb, wooden. To him the incessant rain was beating out a dirge. It hammered on the house; it hammered on anyone out in it; it hammered, hammered, hammered on the shed. In dark despair, Brad felt it was even hammering on his brain. Nothing seemed real any more.

Throughout the rest of the afternoon and all evening he remained in the shed with Bahamas, pushing aside the food his mother brought out to him, paying little attention to her attempts to console him. He sat brooding, gazing miserably at Bahamas and at the tree in the corner that he had trimmed only hours before; going over and over the inescapable fact that come Christmas, only Mike would be there. Bahamas would be sides of beef hung up somewhere to cool. Never again would he be waiting to show the love his gentle heart bore for everyone.

That night the storm began to worsen. Saturday morning the rain came down harder than ever.

Brad got up early and went to the shed, lingering there as long as he could. Then he donned his sou'wester and plodded disconsolately to work at Brian's fishing resort on the riverbank.

On the way, he glanced at the Klamath. That it had risen markedly since the previous afternoon and was bounding seaward in huge swishing rollers, dark with mud, made no impression on his leaden mind. Neither did the fact that Brian's floating dock now rode high. The mooring cables at either end creaked loudly where they looped around the trunks of the big pepperwoods.

In a daze Brad walked into the boathouse. Brian, stirring a can of paint, looked up as Brad opened the door and stumbled in.

"Morning," Brian greeted affably. "She's sure puttin' her down—especially since daylight."

One of the really skilled river guides, Brian Turner was tall, gaunt, Lincolnesque. A man of good will. His deep-set eyes grew keen as they observed the preoccupation of his helper, just then slowly removing his oilskins and hanging them on a peg beside the door.

"Sure comin' down," Brian repeated.

Brad smiled absently and went to the woodstove to warm himself and dry his boots. He said nothing, but spread his hands over the heat and let his empty gaze wander to the rain-pounded window. A few moments later he sat down beside one of the boats and began to paint.

Brian showed no surprise at this. He had already heard about Bahamas. Late the evening before, while out checking for possible flooding, he had seen the lights in the

Hale living room and had stopped in for a friendly chat.
Brad had already gone to bed. So when Brian asked if a
Christmas tree had been put up in the shed yet, Monty
took him out to see it and told him of their need and his
heart-rending decision.

The craggy fisherman frowned and scratched his head
when he learned that Bahamas would have to go. "Kind
of rough on the lad, I'd say. This steer is *some* pet." He
regarded his neighbor with searching eyes.

Monty's jaw muscles knotted. "Yes, he is. That was
my error—ever letting him become one, I mean. I should
have laid the whole business out in dollars and cents to
Brad right at the beginning."

"Didn't you?"

"No, I guess not. Time never seemed right. The darn
calf was so pitiful. It had to be babied for weeks. Wouldn't
of lived otherwise. And Brad kept on spoiling him, on
and on. A steer, for Pete's sake. Something we eat!" Monty
began to breathe heavily.

For a time the men stood without talking.

All the while, serenely chewing his cud, Bahamas had
been gazing from one to the other as though trying to
make out what they were saying. His eyes glowed. When
curiosity at last got the better of laziness, he raised his
hips and heaved up off his knees. Mooing softly, he lum-
bered over to the fishing guide and rubbed against him,
nearly knocking him over. Brian, after recovering his
balance, threw his head back and laughed.

"You're the funniest critter," he said, stroking the hair
on Bahamas' shoulder. "A first look at you makes me
think of matadors and bloodthirsty crowds screaming their
heads off. On second look"—a pause—"on second look, all

I can think of is a little child, kind of wistful and . . . and trusting, I guess you'd say."

Monty's laugh was short and humorless.

Brian contrived a ghost of a smile. "But Bahamas is something to be eaten and Mike isn't. Right?"

Monty slipped a pipe out of his shirt pocket and ran a finger around in the bowl. "I suppose so. But Mike is Brad's transportation. He doesn't just eat and grow fatter. He pays his way."

"And Bahamas won't until he's butchered," Brian countered slowly, inclining his head so he could study Monty's strained expression.

"No, I guess not."

"What a pity. He's a real individual. Mike's only another donkey. I can see your problem and your viewpoint of course, Hale. I just hope the lad can take it. He's young, but he's manly. All the same, I sure do feel sorry for him."

Brian's face was reflecting the same concern now as he watched Brad painting away at the boat bottom, engulfed in his misery, knowing that this was The Day. No doubt Bahamas' last day. Brian sighed and walked slowly over to Brad.

"I know what's troubling you, son," he said, "and believe me, you have my sympathy."

Brad looked up at the kindliness in his friend's face. "Thanks," he murmured.

Brian went on. "I . . . I think your father hopes you'll look at this as a . . . a matter of business. You'll have to, you know, if you ever have a spread of your own."

When Brad did not answer, the fishing guide selected a chunk of wood from the woodpile and, after tossing it into the stove, watched while the flames took hold. Then he sauntered back to his paint can and began to stir again. "Well, maybe something will happen so's you can keep Bahamas," he said in a more hopeful tone.

Brad looked away. "Mr. Everett is coming this morning."

In the hollows beneath his craggy brows, Brian's eyes darkened with pity. "I know," he said. After a moment he opened his mouth to add something, but, apparently deciding against it, shook his head sadly and lapsed into silence.

For nearly an hour the two worked along together. Every so often, obviously aiming to divert Brad's thoughts, Brian turned on the radio for music and news. Since this did not work, he got up and stood by the window, looking out at the Klamath.

"River seems to be rising more and more," he called above the storm's mounting din.

Brad appeared not to have heard him. Brian cleared his throat and tried again. "Believe I'll leave the dock afloat instead of bringing it up on the skids. Those two-inch cables ought to hold her. After all, the pepperwoods she's moored to are over ten feet through."

Because Brian had spoken more forcefully this time, Brad reacted, but only to the sound of Brian's voice, not to what he had said. His blue eyes flickered around the room for a moment. Then he went back to work. Later, having finished painting that particular boat, he laid his brush across the top of the can and slumped in his chair.

The rain continued to pound. The morning turned cold with a bone-chilling dampness. The Weather Bureau extended no hope of early change. Its quarter-hour reports sounded like a broken record: "No relief in sight."

All the while, in the high country behind the tall coastal forests—in the lofty Cascades, the Marble Mountains, the Salmon-Trinity Alps Wilderness, the Siskiyous, the Yolla Bolly, and the Bolly Choop—snow was piling up foot on foot to make the deepest, wettest pack in years.

Inside the warm boathouse Brad, for once, did not ask Brian what he wanted done next. Quite plainly his mind was not on his work. It had drifted off to the rise at the corner of the Hale pasture where, in the shed, Bahamas was probably standing before the manger munching some alfalfa.

All of a sudden Brad stiffened. This evening he would walk into the shed to care for his pets and Bahamas would not be there. Nor would he ever be there again. Only Mike—loud, insensitive Mike. Bahamas would . . .

Brad choked up. Unsteadily, with tears stinging his eyes, he rose and went to the stove. The moment was drawing inexorably nearer when Bahamas would be led from the corral, up the ramp, into a stock trailer, and taken away to slaughter. He glanced at the old-fashioned clock on the boathouse wall. Tick-tock tick-tock, second by second, minute by minute, time was going. Tick-tock tick-tock, on and on, on and on.

Standing beside the stove, rolling a balled fist in the palm of his hand, Brad suddenly thought of something else, and it jolted the breath out of him.

When Mr. Everett walked up to Bahamas that morning he would be welcomed like all other visitors who came. Why, Bahamas would just naturally think of him as another friend. He would expect to have his ears scratched and to be fussed over generally. In return, he would want to sniff noisily around Mr. Everett's face and neck. He couldn't know the stranger intended to lead him to his death!

Brad began pounding his fist into his hand. This must not happen to Bahamas, he told himself desperately. Never, *Never!*

But it was going to happen. Soon, too. He knew this. Somehow he had to act like a man. What if he went to pieces and cried like some little kid! Yet how was he ever going to stand there and see his steer led away? There would be such a terrible finality about his last glimpse of Bahamas.

Any moment now the boathouse phone would ring. His father would be calling for him to come home and talk with Mr. Everett.

With pained eyes Brian watched from the tackle room. Dismay showed in his every movement as he looped a length of towline and flung it onto a shelf. Aloud, he muttered brusquely, "Dear God, can't you figure out something for this lad? He's in such a bad way and he needs help. We sure could use a miracle right now."

But the clock ticked on and on and on through the morning, and the dreary rain kept falling without letup. No miracle presented itself.

Soon after the clock struck eleven, Brian put on his oilskins and stepped out onto the boathouse porch. While watching the river, his attention was drawn skyward. A strong, shifting wind had come up and was driving the rain first one way and then another, in gray, undulating sheets. Already the redwood forests on the mountains across the river loomed dark and blurred and foreboding.

Cloudlike mists enveloped them clear down to the broadleaf trees at their bases, so that in a way they did not appear to be of this earth.

Even as Brian stood there, the Klamath, bounding past, rose higher than ever and its load of silt grew heavier. The muddy water was growing more roily too. And it had taken on a different look, just as the day was beginning to take on a different feel. Something about it made Brian pace back and forth uneasily.

Finally turning away, he let himself into the boathouse and said to Brad, "I believe I'll fix a calibrated measuring stick. Then let's go out and drive it into the bank below here. We better keep track of the rise in the river. I've a hunch we're in for some high water."

Brad nodded and reached for his slicker.

He was making ready to put it on when the telephone on the wall jangled with the nerve-shattering violence of a fire alarm in the dead of night. For a second or two the noise paralyzed him. Then, recognizing the sound and what it meant, he whirled toward it, his fists clenched, his face ashen.

Brian glanced at him and hesitated uncertainly. Having no other choice, he shuffled across the room to answer. "Now, who the devil can that be?" he muttered needlessly.

Brad knew. He knew as surely as if his father had suddenly appeared before him, big, grave, and purposeful. Brad swallowed hard.

With a shaking hand he brushed aside the lock of hair arching over his forehead, and with it, some beads of perspiration. Tense and trembling, he stared at the telephone as if it were some kind of monster.

Brian glanced at him again, wet his lips, and removed the receiver from the hook. He did not sound like himself when he spoke. "Hello. Oh, yes, Hale. Yes, he's here. Hold a minute."

Brad's heart almost stopped beating as he stumbled to the telephone. His fingers, icy and fumbling, took the receiver from Brian. This would be his call, all right. No need to ask if Mr. Everett had arrived.

"Can you come home now, son?" His father's voice was deep and resonant and calm.

Brad replied tonelessly through stiff lips. His voice dropped almost to a whisper. "I . . . I'll be there in a minute."

Misery was etched harshly in his face when he hung up. In a trance he went about getting into his oilskins. While he worked to fasten the chinstrap of his sou'wester, the beating on the boathouse windows began to sound more sharply stacatto, as though gravel, not raindrops, was being hurled against them. It almost drowned out the relentless stroking of the clock pendulum.

At the door, Brad paused. The fishing guide put his arm around his young friend's shoulders sympathetically. "I guess if ever a lad needs to become a man ahead of time, he'll somehow find the courage to be that man," he consoled. "I'll be a-thinkin' about you."

Brad could say nothing. He didn't trust himself enough to even thank Brian. Instead, he merely nodded and made an attempt to smile.

Then he opened the door and stepped out into the swirling rain.

EIGHT

Beans for
Christmas
Dinner

Home was only a short distance away—less than a hundred yards, actually—but today, for Brad, it seemed a mile.

The force of the downpour made walking difficult. Even breathing took effort because of the wind. But most devastating of all was the thought of Bahamas out in the shed, waiting his last for someone to come and see to his comforts.

On the back porch Brad stomped his feet to get the mud off his boots and the water off his oilskins. And to delay going into the house. Finally he straightened and squared his shoulders. At the same time, he looked around, expecting to find the cattle buyer's truck and trailer alongside the corral. He saw neither. Of course! The man had left them in front of the house until he could arrange the . . . the details. White-faced, Brad pulled open the door and crossed the threshold into the warmth of the kitchen.

His haggard glance went immediately to the table with its red-checked cloth and bowls of salad and stew, then to his mother, slicing a loaf of her bread. Odd, how she smiled at him, Brad mused. Well, she probably wanted to bolster his courage. That was Mom. But why lunch an hour early and just as though this were any old day and not the day when . . . when Bahamas . . .

Bewildered, he looked at her for an explanation. He received one promptly.

"Brad, Mr. Everett just phoned," Jane told him, her eyes snapping with excitement. "He can't get here today. The road's washed out."

Brad gasped and stared blankly. The shock was almost too much to absorb. His lips moved soundlessly, repeating his mother's words.

All at once it got through that Mr. Everett actually hadn't come; that Bahamas was safe—for the present, at least.

The dullness in his eyes vanished. With a whoop of joy he tore off his sou'wester and hurled it into the air so hard it slapped the ceiling, left a damp mark there, and sprinkled droplets down on the linoleum. He threw his arms around his mother in a bear hug, then lifted and whirled her around, which he loved doing now that he had grown tall and muscular. It was something he reserved for special celebrations such as her birthday and momentous occasions like this one.

Monty Hale, hands in pockets, almost filled the living-room doorway as he stood watching it all. "You know," he said wryly, "I'll bet I'm more relieved than anyone that we can delay this . . . this thing . . . a bit."

He cleared his throat noisily and, sauntering to the stove, poured himself a mug of hot coffee.

After a sip or two from the steaming mug, Monty went on: "Looks like everything's out of our control. For now, anyway. We aren't going to eat fancy for many a moon, I expect, but I've always thought you fix a mean pot of beans, Jane. Better not mind beans for Christmas dinner, you two, for that's what it's got to be."

"Mind!" Brad shouted, his changing voice shooting up an octave. "Of course we don't mind, do we, Mom? Yowe-e-e-e! Good old beans!"

He snatched his sou'wester off the floor and clapped it onto his touseled head. Without bothering to fasten the chinstrap, he rushed out into the rain toward the corral.

For most of the afternoon Brad stayed out in the shed with Bahamas, currying and brushing him and setting a wave in his winter coat. He found a dozen things to do for his steer—out of the greatest relief he had ever felt. All the while Bahamas absorbed every attention, making small rapturous noises and leaning his half-ton-plus self against Brad until both of them nearly fell over. Finally he bunted Brad with his blunt nose and sent him sprawling.

Later, after Mike had taken a quick run to the end of the pasture, around the stump and back, and had been rubbed dry, the three of them lay in the straw. Brad gazed at the decorated Christmas tree in the corner. Somehow the tinsel and ornaments seemed brighter than before;

the fir more fragrant; the filmy angel on the tip more meaningful. Looking up at her, Brad grinned and tossed a crisp salute.

The rain pounded on and on. If anything, it came down harder than it had that morning, much harder than the day before and the day before that. Brad knew there had to be blowdowns and slides on all the roads.

Toward evening, the Hale's next door neighbor, Gene Fitzpatrick, stopped by. Brad, who had left Mike and Bahamas to sleep away the day's last dreary hours, answered Gene's knock.

The big gruff man, usually so full of wit, saw nothing to joke about this afternoon. Under his dripping sou'wester his face was grave with concern. Clomping to the fireplace and spreading out his hands to warm, he let out a vast breath and wagged his head dolefully.

"If this storm keeps up much longer, we'll have to swim out of here," he predicted.

Monty's tone was terse. "Four o'clock news said more of the same's coming."

"There's got to be a break sometime, Hale. The old Klamath can't take much more of this."

"Lots of gulls around," Monty pointed out. The sea gulls wouldn't be leaving the protection of land until clearing was on the way.

"You noticed the tree frogs?"

"No, why?"

"They're chirpin' their little heads off and shinnying up the trees like their lives depended on it. And you know something?"

"What?"

"Their lives do depend on it. They're tellin' us high water's coming."

"This rain simply can't go on forever," Jane said.

Again Gene shook his head. "Well, it's makin' one all-out try."

Brad had straddled a chair and folded his arms on the back. Although he appeared to be listening, his mind was on something else: What would happen at their house when the storm finally did let up? Because the thought terrified him, he found himself wishing fervently that it would never stop—that it would go on and on.

When he discovered what he was doing, he was ashamed. How well he knew what happened in redwood country whenever winter rains kept up like this. Over and over again he had heard every detail of the great Christmas flood of 1955. And no matter what, once the rains quit, he'd have his tragedy to face. It couldn't possibly be many days now until . . . until, well . . . Brad stared disconsolately at the floor as the three around him talked on.

Soon after Gene left, the storm increased in violence. Dark and troubled, the day drew to a close.

Often now Brad went to see if Mike and Bahamas were all right. Each time he found Mike eating and Bahamas sleeping, both luxuriating in their comforts.

The last trip out, Brad leaned against the wall and watched Mike lie down and stretch his neck until he could scrub Bahamas' face with his long tongue. Brad had to laugh. Even for the delight of Mike's caress, the Angus could not bring himself to open his eyes. But he did manage to rouse just enough to raise his big black head and turn it languidly this way and that so his pal wouldn't miss a single place. Then he lowered it slowly to keep his chin whiskers from being licked the wrong direction.

Mike, eyes mellow with affection, seemed to enjoy all this as much as Bahamas did. When at last he had finished his labor of love, he lipped tentatively at some wisps of straw, sighed with contentment, and flattened out.

Before the donkey could drift off into his nap, Brad squatted down and stroked him. "You old softy," he said fondly, "you'd like people to think you're a hellion, wouldn't you? But you aren't fooling me one bit."

Mike closed his eyes, grunted, and ignored both remarks. Brad chuckled.

Turning back to Bahamas, his face sobered and his thoughts grew desperate. His steer was so dependent, therefore so helpless. Somehow Bahamas had to be saved. There must be a way. There had to be. He'd *have* to find it!

Brad slipped an arm around the steer's neck and pulled the face to him. Bahamas stirred lazily, snuffed once or twice, and buried his nose companionably in Brad's woolly sweater.

The six-o'clock broadcast crackled with reports, none of them good. Every California station carried dire forecasts and warnings. Not only this, but at radio and television stations all over the nation now, the Northwestern storm was turning into the news story of the hour.

The three Hales, listening to their transistor, grew more and more tense. Their situation was worsening.

The announcer's voice came through, hoarse but calm.

"Here's another bulletin just handed me: 'Helicopters have been requested from Hamilton Air Force Base for rescue work and food drops to those stranded in the valleys of the Eel and Mad Rivers and Redwood Creek. Bridges everywhere are going. Only the . . . Klamath and Smith are now reported to be starting to . . . residents had better . . .' "

The voice faded into a snarl of howling and static, then swelled to full volume. "Motorists on the Redwood Highway take refuge . . . will continue to rise . . . towns on the Eel River ordered to evacuate area . . . Rio Del, Pepperwood . . . debris and pressure building up behind the piers of the Klamath's Bear Bridge . . . Requa . . . Klamath Glen be watchful. . . ."

Here, a great crashing sound split the air as somewhere two electric lines swung together and arced.

Jane Hale's eyes widened with awe at the growing magnitude of the storm. "Why Monty, I had no idea!"

"Not our Bear Bridge!" Brad exclaimed. "It'd stand through anything. It stood in fifty-five. It could never go down—"

"What do we do, Monty?" Jane interrupted quietly.

Monty rose faster than he usually did and donned his hard hat and raincoat quickly. "I don't know, Jane," he said, "but I'm sure going to find out."

Seconds later he was gone.

Brad tried to smile at his mother. Before he spoke, he concentrated on making his voice sound strong and confident. "Don't worry, Mom, the river's been up before. We're safe on this end of the Glen. We're higher here, remember? The water won't reach us even if there should be a little flooding up above."

Jane nodded but could not conceal her apprehension.

Brad hoped what he had said was true, but it was obvious to him that his mother didn't think so. Not with all six rivers carrying masses of big trees, crushing bridges and dumping them into the ocean. As he watched her listening to the howl of the Klamath, he could see that she had become more aware of its tremendous power. He knew, too, how she feared the great sky-scraping redwoods everywhere around, swaying dangerously in the rising wind. No one would have to tell her they had already dropped hundreds of limbs the size of ordinary pines; that many of the giants themselves were crashing earthward, taking dozens of lesser trees with them.

The radio blared on: "Keep constant check . . . people in the lowlands had better think about seeking higher ground . . . civil defense . . . completely isolated. . . ."

For a moment Brad chewed his lip and tried to shrug off the uneasiness he felt at their growing peril. He walked his mother over to the fireplace, hoping she could not sense the alarm building up in him.

Again the even, deliberate voice: "The big front is hitting full force now. . . prepare . . ."

They heard no more, for just then Monty's boots clomped heavily onto the back porch. When he burst in, trailing streams of water, his eyes avoided theirs.

Jane would not be put off. She spoke with an insistence he could not sidestep. "Let's have it, Monty—straight."

"Well, things don't look right."

"River still rising, Dad?" Brad queried anxiously.

"Yes, still rising, but there's something else—*something else.*"

In three or four strides he was across the room. Unfastening the neck of his raincoat, he studied the wall barometer.

"What do we have here, anyhow—a tropical storm?" His tone was explosive with astonishment. "Barometer's up, Jane. Up, mind you. It's 30.08. You may not believe this but it's turned *warm.* The wind has shifted to the southwest, and I'll swear it reminds me of the desert wind we felt that time down in Los Angeles. Craziest thing!"

Jane regarded her husband with frank suspicion. Hands on hips, she faced him squarely. "All right, Monty, how bad are things—really?"

Brad watched, his mouth tight. His eyes narrowed as Monty ran a hand restlessly through his hair.

"Well, Jane, I suppose we'd better begin to take our—whatever you want—upstairs. It's possible the river could slip over its banks tonight. But don't worry. I doubt that it will."

Disregarding the evasive replies, Jane probed further. "Monty, what does Brian say?"

On sudden impulse, the big logger threw an arm around his wife's shoulders and smiled down at her. "Now, honey, don't get upset. Brian and some of us are keeping watch all the time. If things get bad, I'll come home and we'll go up to the mill. But I think the banks will hold."

There was no answering smile on Jane's face. Brad could see that although his father had tried his best to be noncommittal, his mother wasn't buying it. Neither was he. How could anyone be convinced the Klamath would stay within banks, that it would not sweep houses, bridges, trees, villages—everything—out to sea?

Brad's uneasiness mounted. There were Mike and Bahamas to consider.

His father's deep voice jolted him from his thoughts.

"Son, you and your mother get things upstairs, will you? And lay out some extra food and clothes. I'll be back after a bit to move any heavy stuff up. We'll play it safe."

With this, he was gone.

While Jane gathered together the silver and other downstairs valuables, Brad raced out to the shed for a few minutes.

Before pushing the door open, he stopped to listen to the river. Could this be the one he had always called "the sweetest salmon and steelhead stream on earth"? It was now a monster, dreadful and frightening. Brad could hear trees tumbling in it, crashing together with woody thuds, colliding with the big boulders also being swept along. And he knew these trees were not only the riverbank alders and willows and tanoaks but also massive redwood giants that had been standing in all their ancient splendor only minutes before.

He scowled up into the rain and darkness, trying to make out the great arms of the pepperwoods spreading overhead. He could not see one, but he could hear their piercing creaks as they whipped wildly in the wind. He shook his head as if to clear it.

Tuned in to the moaning of the forest towering ominously all around him, Brad shuddered. He felt his flesh start to creep.

NINE

Snow Melt and Whole Gale

Night, black and threatening, settled over the Glen as the front, with savage fury, howled in off the Pacific. By midnight the storm had developed into a full-throated gale, slamming torrential rains down onto the already sodden earth, driving rocks into the ground. Hour by hour the fury heightened. Everyone now expected flooding. The only question was how serious it would be and how soon.

While the men kept watch along the river, the women busied themselves with household chores. They carried valuables to second-floor rooms, assembled emergency foodstocks, and kept lights burning both upstairs and down. In many of their windows, lighted Christmas wreathes sparkled; in some of their living rooms, gaily decorated trees. Men patroling in the sopping darkness could look back and see the warm glow and be heartened by it.

Shortly after 2 A.M. Monty came in. Brad could tell that he was trying to appear casual. But his lips were drawn too tightly over his teeth.

"How do things look now?" Jane asked, pouring a mug of coffee.

Before answering, Monty rubbed his face and hair briskly with a heavy towel. His reply was unhurried and deliberate. "River's pretty high."

Brad grimaced impatiently. Of course it was high. Couldn't they hear it less than a hundred feet away, rushing around the bend? They could hear it above the spasmodic thrashing of the maples and pepperwoods and the drumming of rain on the roof.

"Quite a gang down at Turner's," Monty added. "Brian, of course. Gene. Rusty and Clipper. Others from time to time."

Jane handed her husband his coffee. "Thank Heaven for Rusty and Clipper. They've been through this before. They'll know what to do. Besides, they're so . . . so big."

Brad nodded. Both loggers were huge. Standing well over six feet and with enormous arms and shoulders, they were truly the Paul Bunyans of the giant forest. They towered over all the other loggers, even his tall, rugged father, like the redwoods towered above the firs, Brad thought.

"What did Rusty and Clipper say?" he asked his father.

Monty studied the steam rising from his coffee. "Very little. They're keeping an eye on Frog Pond. Water's hitting hard up there."

Brad sensed that his father was trying not to alarm them any more than he had to.

Jane slid her hands into the pockets of her slacks. "What's the river going to do, Monty?"

Monty blew on his coffee. "Boathouse radio says it's going to keep on rising," he said finally.

"When's it to crest?"

"Tomorrow morning about seven."

"How high?"

"Thirty-four feet."

Brad heard his mother gasp slightly.

"What about the Eel?" he asked. He was concerned about the long river to the south—and for a good reason.

Monty hesitated again until, glancing up, he met Brad's intense gaze. "Well, they've about had it. Pacific Lumber has lost its entire cold deck, for one thing. Whole gale warnings have been hoisted all along the coast, so I suppose . . ."

Unable to hold back any longer, Brad broke in. "Dad, is Ferndale all right?" He had to know, because this community at the mouth of the Eel was a rich dairying center.

"Under a good many feet of water," Monty conceded slowly. "The delta's a vast inland sea."

"And the stock?" The question bothering Brad had not been answered.

"Lost a few," Monty admitted. "Mostly those that couldn't get to the hills fast enough, I imagine. Big dairies are probably okay."

Brad's blond brows drew together in a frown. Yes, but what about all the little dairies, he wondered. Those animals feared and hurt and drowned as terribly as the animals of the huge dairies.

He asked no more questions. Staring unhappily into space, he failed to notice that his parents glanced at each other. Neither did he see his father pick up another coffee mug and pour it full. All at once there it was, being held out to him. Brad searched the bold features of his father's face for an explanation. He saw only a half-smile.

Monty's voice was low and vibrant. "We've got to go to the river, son. Better drink up," was all he said.

Brad could only blink with astonishment and reach for the mug.

Never before had he been permitted coffee. He had asked plenty of times, but coffee "for growing boys" had always been one of his father's pet hang-ups. "Don't want to stunt your growth," he had declared. "This jungle brew—the kind that's worth anything—is for full-blown men. When I figure you're about there, you can have it. Not before."

Monty made no more of the occasion than just the pouring, followed by a slight lifting of his own coffee mug in salute. It was as if the mug Brad held were like any other, instead of a milestone in his life. With elaborate unconcern Monty concentrated on his own drink.

Brad threw his mother a glance of surprise and saw that her eyes were moist. Cautiously he took his first swallow of the piping-hot beverage. When the stimulation of it began to course through him, a grin spread over his face.

Afterwards, together, Monty and Brad plodded through the driving rain to the river.

At the boathouse they found the downriver men huddled in a cluster, waiting for Brian and another man to return from upstream.

"It's blowing harder all the time," Monty shouted when he and Brad joined the group.

Everyone nodded but no one answered. Speaking was too difficult. For a few minutes the men stood with hunched shoulders, watching the brownish water bounding past.

That the Klamath was still on the rise was easy to see, for Brian's floating dock rode almost level with the riverbank now. Brad's torch highlighted it out there, pitching and yawing and tearing at its moorings. Around it all kinds of trees were tossed about like broomstraws. Grimly the men studied the roll and tumble of the water thundering past, hissing and splattering high in the air.

Presently two flashlights appeared in the darkness and came bobbing toward them. The group turned and waited expectantly. Brad knew this must be Brian and the other man.

Almost immediately the two stepped into the circle.

The fishing guide stood for a moment, bracing against the wind, one shoulder hunched higher than the other as the downpour bit into that side of his face. His eyes gleamed. "Water's startin' to creep into Charlie Henderson's pasture up at Frog Pond," he said wearily.

Brad's heart took a wild leap. Already—the upper end of the Glen!

No one said anything. Every man waited tensely, swaying in the gusting wind.

Brian went on: "Talked to Tom-Jo Buckeye. He just

now drove in from Klamath. Requa's awash. Boathouse, dock, trailer park, everything down there—gone."

Brad gasped. An entire fishing resort gone? Yes, of course; it had to be. He tried to imagine the wild scene at the mouth of the Klamath, where the tide rushing in was colliding with the torrent pouring out. But . . . but what about them here, pocketed in the big bend of the river? Brad glanced at the set faces all around him and swallowed hard. The premonition gripped him that this was going to be a night to remember.

Suddenly Monty stepped away and played his light over the turbulent water. Brad and the men turned to look with him. Quite definitely, and in the last few minutes, things had worsened. Flashlights were now picking up lumber and cut logs from upstream mills— among them, sections of houses and barns and, for the first time, heavy beams of the kind that make up the under-pinning of bridges. All were bobbing along together in the ugly muddy waves.

Brad was standing beside his father when the body of a bear slipped by between two entangled cedars. Not long afterward a dead cow tumbled past, crushed and bloody. Brad knew the animal had belonged to one of the Indians and had been unable to escape from its riverbar pasture. At the sight of it he recoiled. Caught up in panic, he wheeled and ran for home. For the shed. For Bahamas.

Midway, Brad stopped, disgusted at his headlong flight. Quit acting like a two-year-old and get the heck back there, he told himself. What would the men think, any-how? Especially his father. Monty expected him to face up, otherwise he wouldn't have handed over that first cup of coffee. Humbled, Brad turned and plodded resolutely back to the others and took his place.

When he eased into the group beside Monty, their glances met and held. By the light reflected from a wet raincoat, Brad caught a glimpse of warmth in his father's eyes. Then his attention was drawn to Rusty and Clipper, just then elbowing into the circle. To him, they loomed larger and more capable than ever; their square-jawed faces more like chiseled granite than flesh.

Brian tried to make himself heard above the wind. To the big loggers he shouted, "Comin' up right along. Cuttin' all along the bank here."

"She could roll over it tonight," Clipper said bluntly.

Brian nodded. "Sure could."

Rusty's cold-steel eyes moved from man to man. Rain spattered high from his hard hat and tremendous shoulders as he shifted from one foot to the other restlessly.

When he spoke at last there was decision in his manner. "What do you say we give it another fifteen minutes? If she's still rising, some of us with trucks and jeeps had better get up to Frog Pond and start dragging those house trailers out fast. Ones nearest the river first."

Everyone nodded agreement. Clipper's deep voice now boomed out, "Drag 'em up to the grocery. Pack 'em in tight. Some are big babies. Get them outa the way. That'll leave the high road fairly clear for cars getting out of here."

Again all heads nodded.

Just then a motor was heard and the group turned to see the sheriff's car wallowing through the mud toward them, fanning water from both sides. Brad knew that

Torres and Kentfield, the local deputies, would be in it. By radio they were keeping in constant touch with Crescent City and conditions throughout the area. As soon as they pulled up, the men hurried to them.

Kentfield was a husky fellow with a gravelly voice, and he was using it now. "Still rising?" he shouted.

"Six to eight inches an hour," Brian shouted back.

Both deputies looked serious. Before they could reply, the car radio started blaring. The men outside closed in. Leaning forward, they listened intently.

". . . winds at Freshwater Lagoon now seventy-five miles an hour, southwesterly. Hurricane force hitting all points along the north coast. Advise everyone on the coast and in the river valleys that at any time now . . . repeat: . . ."

The rest of the dispatch was lost in a roaring boom on the slope back of the Glen. The men jumped and whirled around to peer into the drenching rain. While they stood listening, there came a low, sustained rumble, followed by a splintering of wooden timbers.

"That's the old house at the foot of Chimney Tree Trail," Monty shouted. The wind snatched the words and flung them back at him.

The man beside him nodded. "Slope above it has been ready to go for hours. The trail, too. That's it, all right."

Now came another boom, this time from the far side of the river. A big redwood, its roots torn from the earth, had toppled, pulling many other trees with it. The roar bounced across the valley and back again.

The death of the giant was only the beginning. It had triggered destruction for the entire mountainside. The steep slope, rain-soaked and heavy with a dense forest of mammoth trees, rumbled ominously, then gave up. Letting go all at once, the face slipped away from the ancient bedrock and thundered down into the raging torrent below. And when it did, the earth shook as in an earthquake.

Many flashlights illuminated the churning flood. Awed but fascinated, Brad watched the mountain wall break into a hundred chunks, each bearing gigantic redwoods and their understory of lesser trees and shrubs. He saw boulders fly from some that were the size of his bedroom at home. These the bounding water picked up and tossed from one muddy wave to another. In the passing of a few shattering minutes, all vanished as utterly as if they had never existed—the rocks, the soil, the whole forest, and every living thing in it.

The river swelled and bulged. From it rolled a menacing roar. The men looking on were transfixed, their faces gray.

Suddenly, beneath their feet, the ground began to sag. "Jump!" yelled one of the loggers.

They all stumbled backwards. At the same time, the police car ground into gear and leaped away in one splattering lurch. With a moan, the earth where they all had stood collapsed. Like the mountainside across the river, that edge of the Glen was not there any more. It, too, was on its way to the sea.

Torres yelled out the car window, "Watch it, you down here! If . . ." The rest of his words were lost in the fierce gust of wind that whipped the rain directly into the deputy's face and staggered the men outside the car.

After the squall had swept over them, and the police car

had gone, Brad glanced around and saw that every face was grim and drawn.

Scowling, Rusty braced until the wind abated and the buffeting of the pepperwood limbs ceased momentarily. Then he yelled into the huddle of men, "Come on, you upper Glen guys! We start moving. Remember, pull them lower trailers out first." To the fishing guide and the others: "Brian, you folks down here, I don't have to tell you—be ready for anything."

With that, a dozen men headed back into the Glen as fast as the rain and deepening pools of water would let them. Almost instantly they disappeared in the darkness. Those who did not go—Brian, Gene Fitzpatrick, Monty, Brad, and several others—clustered together.

Immediately, Brian turned to his neighbors. In the glow of reflected light he threw Brad a quick, intense look, then pulled Monty aside. "Hale, have you ever given thought to what could happen to Mike and Bahamas if the river should cut across the bend tonight?"

Monty's voice was explosive. *"Cut across the bend!"*

Brian smiled faintly. "Why, sure. You must know it could. It's done it before many times."

Water streamed down their cheeks as the two men measured each other silently. Brad stared, aghast. Over the shoulder of Monty's shining sou'wester he could see Brian watching him sharply, every muscle taut; his face a mask, cold and stark.

Behind them all, the Klamath surged and thundered.

TEN

Disaster

Brad broke and ran for the shed at the high corner of the Hale pasture. His fear was not for himself—he knew he could get out. But Mike and Bahamas—especially Bahamas—how would they ever escape? They had to be taken care of somehow. Brad's heart pounded and his breath came in gasps as he stumbled through the darkness toward the enormous maples and pepperwoods. Toward the lights of home.

He hurled himself against the corral gate, then the shed door. Once inside, he snapped on the light. He stood panting, staring at Bahamas lying in the straw, chewing his cud; and at Mike, standing with his legs stretched wide, tossing his head and showing the whites of his eyes. Brad could see that the donkey was afraid, for he was sweating profusely.

Brad hurried to him and laid a hand firmly on his

quivering rump. "Come on, old boy," he said as confidently as he could. "Easy there. I won't let anything happen to you." He thought he made sense, that he sounded convincing.

Not to Mike, he didn't. Mike opened his mouth, showed his teeth, and blew a loud, troubled breath.

Uncertain about what more he could do for Mike just then, Brad slowly turned away. After a moment he dropped down close to Bahamas and began stroking his neck tentatively. Almost at once little ecstatic noises of pleasure, as relaxed and soothing as the purring of a cat, told him his steer was not a bit excited about the storm. So what if the rain beating on his roof did sound like the drums of a Headhunter jungle rite? For him, the monotony of it had become a lullaby. Contentedly, he lowered his thick lashes and chewed on. He might as well have been lying in the spring wildflowers of his pasture on a sunny April afternoon.

"That's right," Brad said, somewhat relieved. "Just take it easy." He gave the sleek neck another pat or two. Then, as an idea came to him, he stopped and snapped his fingers.

"That's what I'll do," he announced, thinking aloud. "I'll go in and tell Mom I'm going to get my sleeping bag and some food, and ride out the storm with you. Water can't reach *this* high."

His mind made up, he rumpled Bahamas' pile of curls, then scrambled to his feet and headed for the door. Tightening the chinstrap of his sou'wester, he added, "Now, don't worry, you two."

Before he stepped out into the driving rain he glanced

over his shoulder and noted that Bahamas, at least, was following his advice. He didn't appear to be worrying about a thing.

Mike, on the other hand, was stomping back and forth, his eyes rolling first one way and then another. His big ears swiveled in constant search for every sound. To see him so upset wrung Brad's heart.

"I'll be back," he called in a voice intended to allay all fear, "and it won't be long."

It wasn't. Not long at all. But it was the last time he ever would be back.

As Brad plodded across the corral and pulled the gate open, the whine of the wind suddenly swelled to a roar. Then it fell away, although only for the duration of a dozen heartbeats. In those brief moments he heard something that brought him up short. With a groan of despair he stopped and listened.

The night hung heavy with danger and all the terrifying noises that went with it. Yet despite the drumming of rain on his oilskins, Brad picked up a new sound. Even when the wind gusted again he heard it faintly but unmistakably. It was the frantic bawling of cattle.

Everywhere, all over the Glen, they were bawling—family cows in sheds, a few head here and there being hovered by the ground-sweeping skirts of young redwoods. Brad knew what it meant. He knew about animals sensing disaster well before humankind could either hear or see it.

But no bawling came from within his own shed. Bahamas didn't fear a thing. He'd never known what fear

was. The pitiful bellowing of those who had, rocked Brad.
It set him shaking. To steady himself, he gripped one of
the corral posts with both hands and held on so tightly
his flesh went white.

A limb clattering to the ground from one of the pepperwoods jolted him into action. He managed to pull the
gate shut, then ran for the house.

Head lowered against the drenching sheets of rain, he
splashed through water inches deep—rainwater that had
collected because the sodden earth could absorb no more.
He paid no attention. His thoughts centered on one thing:
he must get his mother to fix hot soup in the gallon
Thermos while he made a few sandwiches and gathered
together some gear. The vigil with Mike and Bahamas
might last all the next day. Maybe even into the night.
Wasn't likely to, of course, but it just might.

Since well before midnight, the valley had sounded
like a battlefield. The cannonfire of falling trees was coming from all sides at once. Huge redwoods and firs, ten
to fourteen feet in diameter, bent before the wind until
they snapped or toppled, taking other trees with them.
Added to this bedlam were the booming thuds of giants
that had already tumbled into the angry floodwaters; that
were banging crazily against one another as they leaped
and rolled downstream. And then there was the rush of
streams sluicing through ravines and the thunderous roar
of waterfalls shooting out into space from newly created
gorges on both sides of the river.

At this moment, exactly three-thirty in the morning, the
Klamath was rising faster all the time. Monty and several
of the others, still patroling in front of Brian's place,

hunched inside their raincoats and continued to pace up and down the riverbank, peering out into the seething turmoil.

All at once a pale glow danced over the boathouse. Turning, the men saw headlights approaching. Instead of waiting for the vehicle to pull alongside the building, they moved forward to meet it and closed in around the driver's window as soon as the flying mud would let them. Only then did they see it was the deputies again, Torres at the wheel. Both officers leaned toward them.

Torres scowled into the downpour, his face hard-lined and grave. "Afraid we're going to get it," he shouted against the wind. "Upriver gauge says we're already over the thirty-four-foot crest. Nobody expected it for hours yet."

Brian shot a keen glance at the deputy. "How much now?"

"Thirty-five."

Someone gave a low whistle. One of the men stomped back and forth, muttering. The others shifted nervously.

"Can't take much more," Torres warned.

"You think the river will cut across?" one of the men queried anxiously.

Torres did not hesitate. "I think anything can happen tonight."

"How about Rusty and Clipper and the trailers up at Frog Pond?" someone else asked.

"Trying to keep ahead of the water. They're throwing chains around the trailer tongues and floating them out now. Flood's on their tails all the time."

"What's best to do if we have to evacuate?" Monty said, a huskiness in his voice.

"Try and make it up to the grocery or the mill. Squeeze in wherever you can. You got a camper and four-wheel drive, Hale, so maybe you could try the Old Ridge Road toward Crescent City aways. But move, all of you. Just *move!* And don't plug up the road, any of you guys, whatever you do. One stalled car and we've all had it. We'd never . . ." Torres shook his head. He didn't have to finish.

The officer zoomed the motor once or twice before he shifted. "Get everything you value up high. Be ready to go—in case."

The men nodded and stepped back.

"Be seeing you after a bit," Torres called, rolling up the window. Kentfield tossed a quick wave and the police car sped away, switching from side to side in the mud like a frightened alligator slithering into a swamp.

Before Brian, Monty, and the others could retrace their steps to the riverbank, they heard a yell that seemed to be coming from a distance. Whirling around and peering into the downpour, they saw a flashlight bobbing toward them. In the darkness no one could identify the bearer, but he seemed to be in a terrific hurry.

As he ran up to them and their oilskins reflected the glow of his torch, they recognized Gene Fitzpatrick. Breathlessly he flicked his light from man to man until it came to Monty. "Hale, water's backin' up the other side of our houses!" he rasped.

Immediately all turned to look, forgetting for an instant that they could see nothing beyond the range of their flashbeams except a few house lights.

The river had a tendency to curl back into that corner after making a wide swing around the Glen, especially during floodtimes. Long ago it had fashioned a small peninsula on the lower end of the curve. Now, swiftly moving currents were eddying into the cove, pushing up fast, reaching for the houses on the point.

Gene's voice shook with undisguised alarm. "Water's climbing higher and higher!"

Monty thrust his jaw forward. In the pale light his narrowed eyes gleamed. "How high?"

"Almost to the top of the bank. Don't have far to go."

For a moment the two men stared at each other, both breathing hard. The strongly chiseled planes of their faces shone like polished marble.

All at once the telephone in the boathouse rang with an urgency that commanded instant response. In no more than a dozen long-legged strides, Brian was through the door, snatching the receiver off the hook. Monty rushed in behind him, followed by the others.

Brian's face streamed water. It ran into his mouth and off his chin as he spoke. "Turner here."

"Fire station, Brian. Things look bad. Just got a call from Scotts Bar up in the Trinity. Forest Service says snow's disappeared off all the mountains back of there."

"What!"

"Meltwater hasn't hit them yet, but pretty quick they think."

"*All* the snow?"

"Right. All. Every bit of that big deep pack clear to Mt. Shasta and on beyond into Oregon. Kaput! *Gone!*"

"That can't be."

"Well, it is. Hours ago temperatures up there started climbing up into the sixties. That did it. Snow stopped falling. Been pouring ever since. Pounded the snow to pieces. I guess water's been roaring into every tiny ravine in cascades you can't believe. Brother! Things must be indescribable. Ranger says watch out down here."

"What about the Salmon-Trinity and the Siskiyous and the Marble Mountains and the . . ."

"Snow's gone from there too. Runoff's tearing down-canyon like the hounds of hell. It's going to hit Martins Ferry before long, and when it does, it'll take the bridge out like nothing."

"God!"

The bridge across the gorge at Martins Ferry stood a hundred feet high.

Brian's face blanched. His intense eyes dulled and seemed to recede into the dark pits beneath his bushy brows. He stared vacantly at the floor.

The other men stood motionless, their eyes riveted on Brian, their faces drawn with exhaustion, their shoulders sagging. The voice at the other end of the line had been loud enough for them to hear.

After a short interval, the fireman went on somewhat more calmly. "Better let everyone know, Brian—and fast. There's still some time. Not much though. Maybe twenty, thirty minutes before this hits us. That's all."

"I see." Brian's voice had gone dead. In his eyes was the look of resignation, of defeat.

The other voice rose again. "One last thing."

Visibly shaken, the fishing guide stiffened. "Go ahead."

"Terwer Creek's starting to run wild. Piggyback truck from the mill made it across the bridge a while ago—with its headlights under water. Klamath's thirty-five and a half feet up here now. If it hits thirty-six you'll hear the fire siren—and when you do, get out! Understand? *Leave everything and go!*"

Brian's reply was firm but nearly inaudible. "Yes, Ed. Thanks."

"Good luck!"

The click sounded like the crack of a sledgehammer on a steel spike.

Slowly, wearily, as if his arm were some mechanical thing and no part of him, Brian returned the receiver to its hook. Just as slowly and wearily he raised his eyes and met the penetrating looks of the others.

No one had time to say anything. A sinister groan came rumbling out of the ground. It surged into the floor, through all the men's boot soles, and up the walls of the small wooden structure, shaking it until the tools rattled and fell from their pegs.

The men rushed out onto the porch. Their flashlight beams darted first over the bounding water and then to where the embankment ought to have been. The last time they had checked, it lay some twenty feet from the boathouse. But not any longer. It had vanished completely.

In its place, muddy rapids rolled and tumbled. And a long way out in them, alternately shooting up into the rain and down out of sight in the floodwaters, was Brian's floating dock. The cables that held it screeched like souls demented. Both of the huge pepperwoods to which it was moored shuddered and strained mightily at their root systems. The new edge of the Glen, lying raw and unfamiliar less than a yard from the boathouse steps, was even then crumbling.

As the men stared in dismay, the wind renewed its fury, sweeping up the valley in gale force; whining and howling and wrenching limbs by the hundreds from the trees; hurling them onto housetops and forest floor and into the widening torrent. In ferocious gusts it slammed the rain down on the metallic hard hats of the men clustered on the riverbank.

Out of common need, the men drew together around the fragile security of their flashlights. Their streaming faces were set.

Brian's gaze slid from one to the other. He studied each for a moment as if trying to fix the memory in his mind for all time to come; as if he might not ever see any of them again. And no one could mistake what he was thinking.

With an effort he forced a faint smile and thumped the shoulders on either side of him. His voice was tired, but strong with courage quickly summoned. "I'm afraid this is it, boys. Get going now—and God be with you."

He and Monty and all the others turned then and bolted for home.

ELEVEN

No Time Left

Monty took little notice that the water he plowed through lay ankle deep and moved slowly or that the eerie night had distorted every shadow, magnified every sound, and shaped each into something monstrous. Neither was he conscious of the tortured limbs of the trees whipping and thrashing overhead, although their wailing rose above the roar of the river like the midnight caterwauling of battling tomcats.

At the front steps of home, he splashed to a stop. He must catch his breath. None of this dashing in and scaring Jane and Brad half to death. He'd *walk* up the steps and into the house and be calm about it. But when Monty turned the doorknob, a gust of wind literally blew him into the room. Only by throwing his weight against the door could he force it shut behind him.

The noise brought Brad on the run. Monty could tell by his son's face that his own must be gaunt and haggard;

that despite his efforts to mask concern, the boy had seen dread in his eyes for the first time. To cover up, he jerked off his hard hat and dug his fingers into his thick hair.

Brad appeared to be in a daze. He stood with feet wide apart, arms hanging loosely. His voice came out weak and uncertain. "Dad—I . . . I've *got* to stay with . . ."

In the press of the moment, Monty did not hear him. "Where's your mother, son?" he broke in.

Jane, hurrying into the room, provided the answer.

When she saw Monty making no move to take off his oilskins, her face revealed, without a word being spoken, that she knew the time had come. Absently brushing aside a strand of hair, she walked slowly toward her husband. Her eyes searched his face. "We leave tonight." She said it. She didn't ask.

Monty's gaze softened. He took her hand. "Yes, honey, we do."

As if bracing for the worst, Jane straightened and folded her arms tightly. Monty could see how determined she was to stand tall beside her menfolk.

"You ready?" he asked in a low voice.

Jane nodded. There was only the barest tremor in her reply. "Brad's been busy. He stowed what we'll need in the camper—food, blankets, coats, everything. I told him the *three* of us might have to be . . . to be away overnight."

Fleetingly, Monty wondered why the emphasis on the *three*. How else? Puzzled for an instant, he studied Brad, now popping his knuckles, his face expressionless. Monty felt a sudden sympathy wash through him.

One corner of his mouth curved upward. "Thanks,

son," he said gently. "We'll need every one of those supplies because we . . . we're going to have to go—now."

Brad stared at his father, his eyes widening. *"Now?"* he blurted.

"Yes. It looks as if . . ."

A heavy stomping on the front porch jarred the house. In a deluge of rain and wind, Gene Fitzpatrick burst into the room, so breathless he could say nothing for a few seconds.

Finally he gasped, "Better hit for high ground. The river's jumped the bank up at Frog Pond. It's already under ten feet of water. Radio just said the Klamath's going to crest at fifty feet or more. *Fifty feet!"*

Alarm sprang into Brad's eyes. "Isn't that the height of the Bear Bridge—fifty feet?"

Monty's jaw muscles knotted. He nodded slightly but did not look around at his family.

Gene went on, speaking fast. "Don't lose any time, folks. I've got Christine in the car. Water's almost up to the hub caps—just in the last few minutes. Need some help? Christine'll blow the horn if the water deepens any. Thought you might . . ."

Over the shrilling of the wind they heard the horn— three loud blasts. The signal! Rushing to the door, Gene stopped only to call back. "We'll hold up for you as long as we dare, but hurry! Don't . . ."

He got no further. A terrific sound split the air. Then it mushroomed into a full-throated roar. They all froze where they stood.

Everyone in the valley must have realized this had to

be the death throes of the Old Giant. For unknown ages it had towered over the Glen. Now its time had come. Above the tornadic winds swooping in with the whining shriek of many jets, it could be heard groaning and wrenching loose from the mother soil all its great gnarled roots.

The toppling of the mighty redwood consumed little more than a minute, but for the four in the Hale living room it stretched into an eternity. Down—down—down the giant crashed in frightful crescendo. No use running for safety. In the darkness, who could tell which direction it would fall? Only one thing was certain: it would grind into the earth anything that lay in its long, long, long path.

When at last the big tree hit the forest floor, the buildings in Klamath Glen vibrated like plucked guitar strings, and the requiem for its going echoed and re-echoed from the surrounding mountains. As if in sorrow as well as in tribute to twenty centuries of majesty and grandeur, the lights dipped and nearly went out. Then, gradually, they resumed full strength.

At the same time, rising in the nightmarish bedlam, came a throaty wail. The siren! Like the mournful scream of a banshee, it soared through the hideous night.

For a minute Gene Fitzpatrick and the Hales stood unmoving, stiff with shock, listening. Cold chills coursed up and down their spines. There could be no mistaking what the siren meant.

"Take care!" Gene shouted. "Get on your way!" And he was gone. Before he could pull the door shut behind him, a wave of muddy water rolled over the threshold.

Monty whirled toward his family protectively. "Jane, grab our things. Hurry!" he rasped.

Without a word, she ran to the bedroom to get their suitcase and totebag, long packed and waiting.

Monty turned to his son. "Brad . . ." He stopped. The boy was trembling, staring at him wildly. His fists were clenched at his sides. Every vestige of color had drained from his face.

Reaching out, Monty took hold of his shoulders. "Son," he said kindly, "we're going to have to leave them."

Brad did not answer. He seemed unable to utter a sound. Monty shook him gently. "Come on now, fella. We've got to go. On the double!"

In his misery, Brad spread his hands and appealed in a hoarse whisper. "Dad, Mike and Bahamas can't . . ." His voice trailed off.

Monty did not hesitate. He rushed to the back porch, grabbed Brad's sou'wester, dashed back, and pushed it at him. "Hurry, son. Don't just stand there. We're going to be swamped any minute now. We've got to get up the Old Ridge Road while there's still time."

Brad gaped at him blankly. Then, with a sharp cry, he leaped past Monty, yanked the door open, and, bare-headed, darted out into the storm. As he disappeared into the darkness, the wind roared in, peppering the room with twigs and shredded leaves. With it came a new surge of water. It rolled swiftly across the living-room rug and into the kitchen.

Through the open door, the floor lamp highlighted the evil-looking waves outside. Monty saw them as he stared after Brad. He also saw the water swirling across their front steps and far out in the driving rain; out past the lawn and flower garden; out past the fence and the zigzag path used by the deer to go down to the river. Everywhere, as far as eye could reach, water, angry and malignant, was bounding on and on, seven miles to the sea.

Monty turned and shouted. "Jane, get into the camper —fast! I'll be right back." With that, he snapped on his flashlight and rushed out after his son.

Around the side of the house he ran, plowing through whirlpools, through the terrible hostility of the wind. Water carrying a tremendous load of mud and debris swelled against his legs, almost forcing him back. Once he came close to falling headlong. Somehow recovering himself, he stumbled up the slope and in through the corral gate.

Here there was no flooding. Only mud and lots of it. The water had not yet risen enough to cover the hillock, but before long it would, for it was already beginning to tear ferociously across the Glen.

Through the gloom inside the shed, Monty saw Brad crouched in the straw against Bahamas. Sopping wet, his hair plastered to his head, he was crying convulsively. The sight shook Monty. He hadn't seen the boy cry in years, not even the day he broke his leg. Monty's heart ached for his son and for the doomed animals he loved so much.

Bahamas did not seem to realize that his danger was critical or that there was any danger at all—even with the siren wailing up and down, up and down. Aside from sniffing the wind somewhat apprehensively, he appeared to be as unperturbed as ever; as pleased with Brad's hug of anguish as he had always been with his hugs of affection.

Monty noticed that things were different with Mike. His sides heaved and his eyes bulged with abject terror. Drenched in perspiration, he ran back and forth, snorting. He wasn't fooled. He smelled fear on Monty and Brad.

Suddenly, with a wild scream, Mike panicked. He bolted from the shed. Outside, in the pounding rain, he raced round and round the corral, wheeling and lunging. After him ran Monty, shouting, beating his oilskins with his hands, waving his arms, gradually herding the terrified donkey toward the open gate.

There, Mike reared up on his hind legs. Out in the darkness before him, the water swished and threatened. Again Mike reared up, then again and still again. Screaming and snorting, he pawed the air.

With time going fast, Monty knew he must do the only thing left to him. He gave Mike a sharp slap on the rump. Surprised, the donkey plunged through the gate and into the churning water. Almost instantly he was swallowed up in the utter chaos of the night.

Breathing hard, Monty wiped the water out of his eyes. He tried to catch his breath, all the while peering into the black void into which the donkey had vanished. Mike had headed in the general direction of Chimney Tree Mountain back of the Glen, he noted with relief. Aloud he muttered, "You'll find a high spot. You'll save yourself."

Quickly he spun around and ran back into the shed.

For several moments he stood panting, looking down

at the Angus. Poor gentle critter, he thought, you've been petted by everybody in the valley. Now, because of all the pampering and spoiling, you haven't the spunk to fight for your life. Nothing can save you. You'll stand right here in your own shed and drown.

Monty stooped and grasped Brad's arm. "Brad!" he yelled, trying to make himself heard above the siren. "Come on! We've got to go. We've got to get out of here!"

But Brad was not to be torn from Bahamas. He only clung to him more tightly. And Bahamas went on licking his face and neck as lovingly as he ever had—or ever would again.

Outside, rolling waves began creeping up the knoll toward the corral. The floodwaters were steadily closing in, and not many feet away now.

"Brad!" Monty yelled again, "Brad! We *have* to go!"

Gasping sobs racked the boy. "I . . . I can't," he cried, shaking his head.

"Bahamas'll be all right here," Monty insisted, knowing better. "We'll come back tomorrow. *Come on!*" He yanked Brad to his feet and shook him, then held onto him firmly.

Hands over his face, Brad sobbed as if his heart would break. "What can I say to him?" he moaned, laying bare his torment.

"Say to him!" Monty found himself without words. This was outside his realm of understanding.

"I . . . I can't just . . ."

At a total loss, Monty hesitated. In desperation, his voice rose to a shout. "How do I know what to say to a steer!"

A gust of wind cleared his thoughts. He stopped. His tone softened. "I don't know, son, but say it fast."

Brad broke away from his father's grasp. He flung his arms around the steer's neck. "Bahamas," he cried in a choked voice, "don't be scared. God is all around you. *I know.* He's all around."

Monty did not hear what his son said. He only saw that his lips moved, that he clung to his beloved pet. It jolted him. His control shattered. Roughly he pulled Brad from Bahamas and onto his feet. His lips were taut against his teeth, his voice compelling and urgent.

"Quick! Help me, Brad. For God's sake, help me. Run for the house. See that your mother's in the camper. Get the motor going. Hurry!"

The two stood for a moment, gripping each other's arms. In those few seconds Monty let his great need reach out. Eyes glistening, he now pled silently, man to man.

Brad could not reply. His face gray and set, he tore himself away. A sharp cry escaped him as he leaped into the savage current and went plunging toward the house.

He never looked back.

In the shed, pushing and tugging with the nearly superhuman strength of a logger long accustomed to wrestling big timber, Monty forced Bahamas up onto his feet. But that was as far as he could get him. He tried slapping the rump, the way he had Mike's, thinking to drive him into the open where he'd at least have a chance. But Bahamas saw no reason for such exertion. With a storm howling outside, he liked it right where he was. He did bellow with surprise, though, at being struck so rudely.

No one had ever done this to him before. He looked as if his feelings were hurt. Certainly his rump smarted.

Suddenly Monty heard the car start. Then he heard it sputter and quit. He rushed to the doorway. The motor turned over again, slowly, laboriously, faltered—and quit. A third time the motor turned over and over and over. All at once it took hold. An instant later the headlights came on. In their glow, Monty could see filthy brown water boiling up over the bumper.

Dashing back to Bahamas, he tried to shove him out into the corral, but the steer only rolled his eyes in wonder—and remained exactly where he was.

Just then the river started lapping at the corral posts.

Between screams of the siren Monty heard the car horn blow. It made him gasp. He pressed his lips together. His flashlight beam swept over Bahamas and into the corner—to the little Christmas tree and the filmy angel with arms outstretched on its tip.

Again Monty swatted Bahamas. This time he shouted as loudly as he could. Once more the animal, somewhat startled, merely looked at him—and went on chewing his cud.

With a groan, Monty turned on his heel and ran from the shed.

Out in the corral he stopped long enough to kick down a length of fencing. Then, through the fury of the gale and the angry rising water, he stumbled toward the camper.

Left behind in the darkness, Bahamas stood alone in the ever-growing terror of redwood country's "Thousand Year Storm."

TWELVE

Journey
into Fear

Not five minutes after Brad and his parents had driven away through engine-deep water and slashing rain, a big wild redwood log crashed through their home. With it came a jam of other debris—uprooted trees and great chunks of underbrush matted together. All this the house could not withstand. Its lights flickered and went out. Then it crumbled. At the Hale place blackness was total.

There was no stopping the rampage of the mighty Klamath. As the front moved in off the Pacific, the monster river leaped the bend. At half a million cubic feet per second, it began carving a new channel.

Through all the buildings and down all the streets of Klamath Glen it tore in savage torrent, wrenching loose everything it struck.

Above the screaming of the hurricane-force winds came the din of stores and houses and barns slamming crazily into one another, crumpling before the onslaught. Like a maniac the muddy deluge rolled over the village, engulfing it completely. No headlights turned into it now. There remained only one possible direction for anyone still able to move, and that was out. Every living thing unable to make its way to safety faced certain death.

For a few minutes the knoll with its corral and shed stood above water. But not for long. The clatter of the Hale camper had scarcely died away before the roily water tossed a dead fish into the corral mud. Minutes after that, a huge Douglas fir ripped out one whole side of fencing and shoved it into the current.

Inside the shed Bahamas was becoming more and more agitated. He had never heard so many strange and threatening sounds. Instinctively he backed into the far corner next to his Christmas tree, where he could be more protected. Even so, the wind howled in through the open door, driving sheets of rain before it. Sudden gusts swirled into every niche. They shook loose some of the ornaments Brad had hung on the boughs of the little fir and rolled them around in the straw and on the dirt floor. Bahamas stepped on several, crushing them. This startled him and added to his growing fears. He turned this way and that, bawling loudly. Where was his family? Why didn't they come? And where was Mike?

Lumbering cautiously to the door again, Bahamas braved the wind and rain long enough to look out, but he could see nothing except bobbing lights in the distance. He was fast becoming aware of water surging through the corral. Before he could retreat into his corner, it had splashed against the shed beside him and splattered up into his face. In mounting alarm he bawled and trotted back to the comfort and security of his straw.

Bahamas found the straw no longer dry. While he had been peering out his doorway, muddy rivulets had run in through the cracks between the boards. They were beginning to move his bedding toward the other side of the shed.

And the noise! Now he was alert to every bit of it—the roar of the water, the grinding together of boulders, the shrilling of the wind, the booming of great redwoods as they fell across one another.

The swollen river had already scoured the valleys and canyons of high country above. Now it cut across its curves, bringing down whole mountainsides of dense primeval forests. Through the deep clefts of the Salmon, the Shasta, the Scott, the Trinity, and on below into the Klamath vaulted thundering floodwaters at express-train speed. In a few wild hours they would avalanche through every gorge, ripping away perpendicular walls that had taken millions of years to form.

Here in the wider basin of the Lower Klamath the water was spreading out, reaching for higher and higher ground, licking at that very minute at the rough siding of the shed atop the knoll.

When Bahamas heard it, he let out a loud bellow— the loudest bellow he had ever let out. Then he waited, soaking wet, trembling.

No happy shout came in answer to his call, no screen door slammed, no boy came running to soothe and calm him.

Out in the darkness, where a pleasant home had stood, only a portion of one wall remained. Everywhere around it was a black void and a sea of tumbling water.

Fear enveloped Bahamas. Forlorn and shivering in his terror, he bellowed again. And again only the whine of the wind in the pepperwoods answered. His animal instinct must have told him his family had fled, that he had been abandoned and was facing death alone.

The river now rapidly crossed the corral—or, rather, where the corral had been. The enclosure had disappeared. Nothing was left of it except the post that held the gate, and the gate had swung wide.

Seconds later the flood flowed in through the open door of the shed and began to swirl around Bahamas' hoofs. Its wetness made him snort and raise his head, as if the doing would lift him out of it.

For many minutes the siren wailed. Then it stopped. No longer were there any sounds that humankind could make in Klamath Glen. No one remained behind to make them.

After the floodwater had covered Bahamas' hoofs, it started pulling at his legs. Panicking, he twisted and turned and sloshed toward the open doorway, only to be driven back to his Christmas tree. His eyes bulged with dread of the unknown and sinister.

As he stood there bellowing, the water rose higher and higher, until it lapped at his belly. The chill caused him to gasp. He had scarcely got his breath back from the shock of it than he began to feel buoyant. Bahamas was slowly being lifted off the ground.

Struggling mightily, he pawed at the dirty waves tugging at him. But they were stronger than he. Nothing could deny the frightful force that had quarried stone cliffs into house-size boulders and was tumbling them downstream.

When the torrent spread out over Klamath Glen, it picked Bahamas up as if he were no more than a leaf from one of the big pepperwoods and swept him out of the corral.

The terrified steer could no longer bellow for help. Swells of water and muddy spray kept leaping into his face. Besides, he was being dragged into deeper and rougher water.

Almost immediately the river flung him into the grotesque corpse of a tanbark oak. The blow knocked the wind out of him and filled his mouth and nose with silt. He coughed and snorted to clear his air passages and get his breath back. Bahamas had never swum before in his life; yet somehow he knew that he must thrash around and keep afloat in the mass of wreckage rushing downriver.

From his home in Klamath Glen, the flood carried Bahamas into the main channel of the river. There the current plucked him from the tanoak and hurled him into the branches of a cedar. Soon a big fir came along. It pushed him under, rolled on top of him, and held him until he almost lost consciousness.

After the fir moved on, Bahamas rose, gasping. He stretched his neck and tried frantically to keep his nose above water.

All around him floated trees of every kind. Most had

been undercut by the flood and toppled into it. The water was a seething mass of them. The roots of many still clung to chunks of the earth in which they had grown and to the underbrush they had shaded. Like enormous corks they bobbed toward the sea.

Among them floated other debris. Gliding and bucking along went both logs and lumber from sawmills up at Orleans and Happy Camp and Hoopa and Siskiyou, miles and miles and countless twists and turns above the Glen. Now and then dead animals and pieces of houses and barns appeared, and even the steel girders of bridges. In the turbulent river was whatever had lain in its path or had not been fleet enough to escape.

Suddenly the current sent Bahamas spinning into the brownish froth that eddied around a stump. Shoved beneath it, he bumped and scraped along the underside. Finally he came up, blinded and choking, fighting to survive.

Gradually his eyes cleared. In a daze he looked around. Daylight had begun to spread a gray wash over the tortured landscape.

All at once Bahamas heard a familiar barnyard voice. In the dreary dawn he saw a rooster riding an outbuilding. As it bounced past and on downstream, the rooster kept craning its scrawny neck into the downpour and crowing hoarsely.

Bahamas had scarcely glimpsed the rooster before being dashed against a snag, the wind knocked out of him. In the ensuing struggle to regain his breath, he lunged toward a patch of small trees; with his forelegs he hooked onto the matting of limbs and foliage. He pulled himself onto it. The next moment he was swept around a curve in the river and toward the sea.

Now Bahamas heard a snorting noise. Turning his head, he saw a huge bear wobbling toward him on a pitching log. Somehow the bear managed to keep his balance, although not for long. He was no surfer. The log gave a vicious lurch and the animal, like a tossed coin, flipped into the air. He plunged down among the twisted branches. There he clung, noisily snorting water out of his nostrils. Seeing Bahamas, he edged closer. For a time the two sniffed nose to nose.

Then something came shooting up out of the depths and struck the bear. A loud grunt burst from his throat. His eyes glazed over. With no more than a low moan, he slid beneath the murky waters and vanished.

Once more Bahamas was alone.

The gale howled on. Driven by the hurricane-force winds, the rain continued to pound the earth, tearing it to pieces, creating a vast wasteland of water.

Not in the memory of man had there been anything like it.

THIRTEEN

Struggle
for
Survival

Bahamas hugged the brushy mass more tightly, bellowing his fear. The river had begun to suck him into a huge whirlpool. It spun him round and round, nauseating him. He retched. Afterward, limp and spent, he laid his head upon the dripping leaves and, for a moment, blacked out.

Then some whimpering noises pulled him back to consciousness. Opening his eyes, he saw nearby a coon and a fox balancing themselves on the same log. They were trying to inch their way toward the riverbank. Bahamas managed a faint bellow in their direction, but in the howling wind and the roaring of the river they did not hear.

As the floodwaters swept all of them around another bend, Bahamas watched the coon and fox spring nimbly from the log to a battered fir. Wobbling along, clinging to the rough bark, they angled toward shore until at last both came to the jagged end of the tree. There they huddled together, teetering precariously, every muscle tensed for that instant of their leap to safety.

The instant came. The two jumped, although not very well, for the fir was bucking and rolling. Miraculously they landed on the embankment. But under the impact of their bodies, the rain-softened earth crumbled and fell away, taking them with it.

Down, down, down they slid, legs flailing among the clods of mud. In their desperation to keep from being swallowed up after all, the fox and coon clawed wildly at the soil and grasses. Barely in time, they braked their descent enough so that they could start scrambling up the riverbank. Bodies aquiver with urgency and waning strength, they were able to pull themselves up over the brink. There they both collapsed, their flanks heaving convulsively.

Bahamas watched this life-and-death struggle until the gray sheets of rain grew thicker, shutting out even the dark redwood forests.

Just as Bahamas' slender short legs began struggling to draw him more securely to the brush, the five arches of the Bear Bridge at Klamath loomed into view. The marvel of concrete and steel, however, meant nothing to him. He had never before seen a bridge.

This one could not really be called a bridge any more. The flotsam of 16,000 square miles of lofty wilderness was gradually crushing it. Great debris jams had already backed up behind its piers. Rolling water was even then reaching with greedy fingers for the deck, normally fifty feet above the water—now less than a dozen.

Huge trees and logs slammed into the pile-up. Some struck in such a way that they glanced off. Like arrows they shot in soaring arcs over the top of the bridge, ripping away sections of the railings as they went. The magnificent structure, pride of the northland, had withstood many ordeals in its time. This storm it would not. Twenty-four hours later, in fifty-five feet of water, it gave way. Klamath's evacuated citizens, secure on the hillside above, heard it go and their eyes brimmed with unashamed tears.

With dizzying speed, Bahamas was borne toward the rubble accumulating at the bridge. All at once the current flung his raft into the jam back of the center pier. The blow hurled Bahamas into some manzanita bushes that had become wedged in an apple tree. Their woody stems were tough and strong and they held him up.

For a time he could do nothing but hang there, blinded, half stunned, gasping. At last the repeated splashing of water on his face washed the mud from his eyes and slapped the cobwebs from his brain. He was shocked into breathing once more.

As his senses sharpened, he tried to pull himself up over the scraggly manzanita branches. But they were too slippery. Bahamas, drained of all his strength, fell back into the water.

Then he saw a small house moving downstream toward the bridge. Toward him. It tilted at an angle as if one side were heavily weighted. The pointed spike of a treetop protruded grotesquely skyward from a window on the opposite side. A mammoth redwood had rammed diagonally up through the floor from somewhere in the depths of the river, and the giant's huge root butt, acting as a brake, was dragging along the bottom, over forty feet below.

While Bahamas watched, the battered house passed

near him. Almost submerged, it slid under the bridge. From there it roller-coastered seaward, disappearing in the fog and low clouds that shrouded the mouth of the river, less than a mile beyond.

The house had scarcely vanished when Bahamas saw another house coming. This one, much larger, drifted closer to him than had the other. It was a two-story farmhouse, the old-fashioned kind: white with gingerbread work along the eaves and a turret tipped with a red arrow weathervane. The old house rode surprisingly high in the water and was not alone in its final hour.

Astride the roof beam stood a donkey. To brace himself, he had spread all four legs far apart, two on each side of the ridgepole. Stretching his head and long neck upward and outward, he kept braying lustily into the pelting rain. The donkey was terror stricken. Mike.

Bahamas heard the gravelly voice and came alive. Desperately he attempted to leap out of the water. In doing so, he almost lost his precious hold on the manzanita. Try as he might, he could not muster any voice with which to respond to those rough-edged heehaws of distress, for he had grown too weak to make a sound of any kind. Bahamas could only watch while the big house with its donkey aboard pitched and lunged in the bounding water —and headed for the bridge.

Mike had to be expert to ride the flood on that housetop. Up there was his only chance of outwitting the Klamath. And it was no mere matching of wits and skill. It was a fight to the finish, a gamble with survival as the stake. In struggling to save himself, Mike had climbed to the loftiest spot he could reach. In this, his moment of glory, he was nothing less than majestic.

Mike did his best, but he was not destined to be one of those to live through the disaster. With a resounding crash the big house plowed into the bridge. It split apart and shattered while Mike was at his vocal best, his brays blasting futilely through the howl of the river, through the shriek of the gale. And he was never seen again.

For a few minutes the rain stopped. Above the bridge the storm clouds broke. As if in benediction, light, pale and silvery, bathed the gloom. Then it vanished. Once again the clouds locked together at treetop level and the sky beat down upon the land as it must have in the time of the Ark.

Panic had gripped Bahamas when the big house hit the bridge. Planks and bricks and furniture had showered all over the water. A chair broke across his shoulders, almost dislodging him from the drift. Yet, after all the fragments had been swallowed up in the sloshing waves, he was still there, clinging to the jam behind the pier and breathing hard from the effort.

At the same time, at the northern end of the bridge, an ugly sea of water and wreckage was fast obliterating the little village of Klamath.

In the titanic crush of the river, large mobile homes became like strips of tin. Swept from their moorings, they wrapped themselves around one another. Dwellings and churches and stores, pushed off their foundations, tumbled about like so many toys. Finally, all to be seen at the Klamath townsite was a roof or two and here and there a television aerial protruding above the swirling mass.

While Bahamas dangled on one edge of his patch of brush, several small fishing boats washed by. Among

them "sinkers" appeared—stumps too heavy to float far
ordinarily. These bumped and ground together and from
time to time prodded Bahamas, bruising him.

Then something jostled his floating island, nearly
swamping it. Bahamas was cast loose. Water closed over
his head.

When he surfaced, he came up dazed and shaken. He
knew only that he was moving. He snorted and gasped
for breath and struck out with his front legs in frantic
attempt to hook onto his manzanita bushes. But they were
not there any more. They had been wrenched apart and
scattered in all directions by a huge tanoak.

So once again the river had Bahamas. With breath-
taking speed it whisked him around the concrete pier into
the tumult below the Bear Bridge. At the same time,
debris pressed in around him. Squeezed between two run-
away logs, the floundering steer caromed on downstream
until the current thrust the strange battering ram into a
big wave. The impact set Bahamas free. Both logs raced
on, leaving him to struggle in their wake.

Seconds later Bahamas mounted the steep slope of another big wave. This one was different. It tasted not only
of dirt, but of salt as well.

Wallowing helplessly in the deep valley of its trough,
Bahamas found himself unable to keep afloat any longer,
and he sank. By some miracle this did not finish him. He
bobbed to the surface. Before he had time to get his
breath, he was pulled into a wind-driven swell so powerful
that it tossed him clear of the water.

He landed squarely in the middle of a huge tangle of

willows and red alders. Only moments before, the trees
had been growing on the embankment at Klamath.

Utterly exhausted, gasping, and in pain, Bahamas lay
in a half-stupor among the branches and foliage. He gave
no sign that he heard a tractor, upside down, smashing
into his haven and shearing off a chunk. Neither did he
appear to notice the body of a she-cougar dangling from
one of the willow poles.

Bahamas was now being swept into what had been the
estuary at the river's mouth. The estuary and its protecting arm, the sandbar, could not be seen this day. A seething desolation of muddy water and debris more than a
mile wide covered both. And into it rolled great ocean
combers, set squarely on collision course with the Klamath. Where they swelled and surged against the ram-
paging torrent, the surf was as steep-sided and monstrous
and cruel as any surf in the world.

Atop the bluffs on either side the wind screamed seventy
miles an hour. Against the jagged rocks below the sea
thundered mightily. Brown foam, torn from the crests
of the breakers, shot up into the fog that concealed the
radar station on the point. The earth trembled with the
shock, and the muffled boom could be heard for miles.

Still limp on his creaking mass of brush, Bahamas was
suddenly startled by a noise—not loud, but unearthly
and terrifying. It frightened him into raising his head. To
his horror he beheld an awesome form rising ghostly and
dripping from the billowing water.

In the sheets of rain the thing appeared to be a phan-
tom. Yet it was real—an enormous redwood from one of
the groves upstream. During the centuries since the birth

of Christ, the giant had grown into a forest monarch wide enough to have filled any road in Klamath Glen; tall enough to have topped the Statue of Liberty; straight-grained enough to have provided the lumber for at least twenty houses.

Now, in all its splendor, the giant shouldered up through mountainous waves. In last salute to its ancestral homeland, the tree rose up and up. At full height, finally, it towered over the ugliness everywhere around as grandly as if it were still standing in the forest among its own kind.

The triumph was brief, the surrender to river and wind and sea all too swift. With a long sigh, and like a sinking ocean liner, the old redwood glided into its watery grave and disappeared.

Paralyzed with fear, Bahamas watched until his eyelids grew heavy and his head dropped into the nest of glistening branches and leaves that cradled him.

He moved no more.

He did not hear the crunch of the big pepperwood and the twisted madrone crowding in among the brush. He could not see that he was being thrust headlong into the boiling surf. Mercifully, he never knew when the maddened Klamath, in bursting wildly from the continent, spewed everything it bore into the vastness of the storm-tossed Pacific. By then he was beyond hearing or seeing or knowing anything.

FOURTEEN

Three Days Later

Three days later, thirty miles northward from the mouth of the Klamath, the coastal village of Crescent City awakened to a bleak Christmas Eve morning. With scream and roar, both wind and waves fell upon the crescent-shaped harbor as the big front in all its fury continued to howl in off the sea.

Both the breakwater and bay inside the jetties had become a solid mass of flotsam. Wedged tightly among huge redwoods and milled lumber and fragments of dwellings and possessions were dozens of commercial fishing vessels—salmon trollers, crabbers, and shrimpers. Beyond them, on out past the lighthouse as far as eye could reach, logs by the thousands floated aimlessly at the whim of wind and current. With each new tide came a fresh and abundant supply. It telescoped the mass already grinding around in the harbor. A pile of giant jackstraws covered the sand for a city block inland from the water's edge.

For a time, that dreary Christmas Eve morning, some men of the shellfish company on Citizens' Dock walked the pier, glumly surveying the wreckage.

"Will you just look at *that!*" one of them exclaimed.

Shaking their heads in despair, the fishermen turned away. They shuffled into the stuffy dock office, took off their foul-weather gear, and gathered around the wood-stove to warm and dry themselves.

No one said anything for some moments. Finally a grizzled giant named Angelo broke the silence. "Never remember a gale like this'n," he said. His remarks set off a rush of conversation.

"Radio says thousands are flooded out. Damage in the millions."

"Yeah. Beaches southa here are covered with dead cattle and sheep and such. Hundreds of 'em. Hundreds! Poor critters drowned in their corrals and barns, then washed into the sea."

"Old Eel River must be a-snortin'," a fisherman called Rogers offered.

"Klamath too."

"That's for sure. Too bad about Klamath and the Glen and Requa. Scun clean off the map."

A solemn-faced man turned to toast his back. "Guess all the Glen folks are still marooned up at the grocery and mill."

"All but the red and white camper that's stuck on the Old Ridge Road," someone put in. "Fellow headed for the

Forest Service cabin, I suppose. Didn't quite make it. Man, wife, teen-age boy."

Kerry, the only youth in the group, was quick to reply. "Buck says they walked to the cabin, though. He dropped food from his 'copter there yestiday."

Angelo scratched his head vigorously. "Good thing. You can bet your last dime they're goin' to be there a while yet. No way to get down. Bracketed by windfalls."

Just then the door burst open and a figure in yellow oilskins ducked in fast. Yanking off his sou'wester, he hurried to the stove, rubbing his hands together. "Man, it's getting cold! I smell snow."

This brought out groans all around. A burly skipper, Krug, turned on the speaker as if he meant to hold him personally responsible for any worsening of the weather. Every hair of his thick butch seemed to stiffen with indignation. "Hey now, we can't have that too!" he blustered.

All the men laughed, although without mirth, for this was no joking matter.

Giving Krug a friendly poke on the shoulder, a dark-haired hulk of a man in a heavy red plaid shirt left the warmth of the stove and strolled to the window for a look outside. He was Don Ford, manager of the company. As Don scanned the drift with their boats embedded in it, he fell to rubbing his mustache thoughtfully.

Conversation lagged for a while. The downpour was beating too hard on the roof of the office for easy talk. The men were content merely to warm themselves and think their thoughts rather than voice them.

One of their number, a swarthy Indian named Jess Grover, left the circle and joined Don. Together they gazed out the window at their boats crunching around in the harbor debris.

"How do you suppose the boys are getting along with the *Sea Belle?*" Jess mused, peering shoreward through the steamed-up glass. He nodded toward the thirty-eight-foot salmon troller that had been tossed far ashore and trapped in the top of the driftwood. Early that morning the vessel's owners, Slim and Bart, had climbed up through the debris to see what could be done. So far they hadn't come in to get dry and report.

"They'll get the boat out, Jess," Don assured him quietly, wiping some steam off the window with the palm of his hand.

"From way back up there?"

"Yup. I think so."

"How?"

Don shrugged. "You know Slim and Bart. They'll find a way."

Jess cocked his head in disbelief but said nothing.

Presently the downpour slackened to no more than a steady drizzle, although clouds, blue-black and threatening, continued to hug the treetops behind the town. Dejectedly the two fishermen at the window scanned the tremendous pile-up ashore and, in it, in the distance, the stranded salmon troller.

All at once Don shot a sidelong glance at Jess. "Rain's eased off," he said in a low tone. "Come on, let's you and me take a quick run to the *Belle* before it starts to pour again."

The Indian nodded and began zipping up his mackinaw.

Outside, in the piercing cold of the morning, both men shuddered. Don almost went back for his jacket but decided not to. They wouldn't be gone long so why weigh himself down with gear? Hands rammed deep in pockets, shoulders hunched, the two set out briskly for shore.

As they strode past the café at the head of the pier, Don tossed the waitress a friendly wave. "Be back inside ten minutes," he shouted. "Put the pot on."

She smiled and formed "okay" with her lips, then headed for the coffeemaker, apron bow bobbing.

From the ramp the fishermen jumped down into the sand and loped along the beach behind the upper edge of the debris. Ahead, hung up in the top of the drift, was the *Sea Belle.*

Before they could climb to a point directly beneath the boat, a bone-chilling wind had whipped up another squall. Rain thundered down upon the debris and splashed in every direction. In no time Don and Jess were soaked. The hull of the *Sea Belle* and the crisscrossed trees and logs upon which it rested did offer some shelter. Here the men braced themselves against a splintered Douglas fir and wiped the water off their faces. Breathing heavily, Don pushed aside some strands of wet hair that kept draining into his eyes.

Jess kicked a chunk of loose bar'- into the sand a dozen feet below, scowled up into the deluge, and pounded the boat bottom with his fists. "Hey! Hey up there!" he yelled.

Almost immediately two deeply seamed faces appeared at the railing. For a few seconds Slim and Bart stared open-mouthed at their unexpected visitors. Then they extended gnarled hands of welcome over the side. Bart's voice boomed. "Hiya! Climb up here before you drown."

As a team, the two brothers worked together perfectly. Whenever confronted with a knotty situation, one of them, with a few bold strokes of a pencil stub on anything handy, would sketch the problem as he saw it. A huddle over the sketch always followed, and from the huddle a workable solution to the problem. In the *Sea Belle's* wheelhouse that morning Slim and Bart had huddled over a salvage plan.

Slim showed Don and Jess the diagram they had drawn on a bit of water-smoothed driftwood from the vast supply outside. Strong pencil lines indicated how they intended to construct a long ramp and sled upon which to ease the troller over the mass of giant driftwood and down to salt water.

"This I have to see," said Don with feeling.

Slim rapped his pipe against the bulkhead to empty it of ashes. "You will," he promised soberly.

Jess raised an eyebrow at Bart.

"Well, why not?" the other retorted good-naturedly. "There's enough solid lumber around here to crate the Pacific Fleet. Must be several million board feet on the drift and out in the harbor. We'll poke around until we find what we need for the ramp and sled. Then we'll build them on the spot." Bart's eyes flashed with confidence.

Don and Jess were wet and cold. Besides, they could almost smell the coffee brewing at the café. As soon as the rain let up, they dropped over the side of the *Sea Belle* and started to work their way along a huge redwood log.

Halfway, Don stopped to gaze at the whole dreary pano-

rama. The sight fascinated him. Without taking his eyes
from it, he shouted over his shoulder. "Jess, hold up a
minute. Come back here and take a look. This is the
darndest thing."

Grumbling something about breakfast, Jess cautiously
edged over to his friend. The two braced themselves and
peered through the fine drizzle sifting down. From their
vantage point, they could survey the greatest field of
driftwood either of them had ever seen. Neither man
spoke for a time. Finally Don said, "You can't even tell
where the beach ends and the bay begins."

"And the stuff just keeps coming, crowding and jam-
ming in like the whole ocean's packed full. When's it
ever going to stop?"

Don took a deep breath. "Who knows!"

"See out there by the harbor lights? Looks like kelp
beds, don't it? Those patches of drift must be hundreds
of feet across."

"And watch those big redwoods shooting over the
breakwater. Man! It takes some sea to do that."

"Never've seen wilder. Never. Not in my twenty years
on fishin' boats," Jess declared.

Don steadied himself in the gusting wind and pointed
to a brushy mass just offshore that was rising and falling
with the swell. "Look at the crooked limb sticking up
out of that tangle of brush. The one that looks like it's
beckoning to us."

"Brush? Where?"

"Way out there—to the right of the white church
steeple with the cross. See?"

"Yeah, I do. How do you suppose that clump ever rode
out the pounding? Where'd it come from?"

"Some river had to have dumped it. The Eel. The Klamath maybe."

Jess was incredulous. "You mean the sea then brought it more than thirty miles upcoast? In *this* storm? Oh, come *on!*"

Don seemed not to have heard the other's gentle sarcasm. He was standing motionless, his eyes still fixed on the strange raft. When at last he spoke, his voice tightened. "Jess, I . . . I think there's something moving in that patch. Something black. Something alive."

Jess laughed. "Oh sure, I bet. Don't you know a cormorant by now, boy? Don't you know that nuthin' but a seagoing bird could possibly be alive out there? I doubt even them."

Wagging his head as if Don had lost his reason, he turned away. "Me for coffee and dry clothes."

When he went to drop down upon an alder, Don grabbed his arm. "Wait, Jess. You may be right. Probably are. But look out there again, will you? That's no cormorant. Yet doesn't it look like something alive?"

The Indian threw him a long, searching glance. Then, apparently deciding to humor his friend, he smiled patiently and, without exerting himself too much, concentrated on the patch of trees and brush out in the bay.

Suddenly Jess bent forward, his eyes squinting intently. Astonishment washed over his face. A moment later surprise exploded. "Well, by jumping golly, there sure as the devil *is* something in that brush and stuff!"

"I'll swear there is," Don exclaimed, a tremor in his voice betraying a mounting excitement. "Come on. Let's go find out!"

FIFTEEN

All
Around Him

Both men glanced around quickly to see how they might climb over the acres of rubble that stretched between them and the object in the patch of brush. All of it would be dangerous going. Don thought he saw a safe route to try.

"This way, Jess," he suggested, warily testing one of the logs that lay across a shattered tanoak. He found the log solid, so from it he boosted himself onto another. Close behind him came his friend.

Carefully, a step at a time, here and there stumbling, the two eventually traversed the debris. They had to pull themselves over redwoods, some of which were ten to fifteen feet in diameter and no doubt washed from a stately grove that had been preserved as a park. Once Don fell with a thud across a section of barn door. "Got to be more careful," he growled, freeing himself from a branch stub that had snagged his jacket.

"Watch out or you'll bust yourself," Jess shouted into the wind, and got a mouthful of rain for his efforts.

After that both men inched along silently, saving their energy for the necessary gymnastics of crawling over the piled-up debris of towns and farms and forests. Repeatedly they were gouged by nails protruding from boards, and skinned by rough bark. Every few minutes the two had to stop to recover their breath and wipe the water out of their eyes. Don and Jess began to think they were never going to reach the black thing in the harbor—progress was so agonizingly slow.

Once, seeking shelter under an overhanging fir, they noticed for the first time a number of oilskin-clad men huddled together on the dock, watching them; Slim and Bart, too, at the rail of the *Sea Belle.*

Jess grinned. "What do you bet the boys are saying that we've lost our wits, climbing all over this stuff toward the bay like we are? Why else would we be doing this in the wind and rain? Can't you just hear them?"

Don had to laugh. "Well, maybe we'd better put their minds to rest," he said. "Anyway, we may need their help if this . . . whatever it is . . . turns out to be alive." He stood up and waved to show that he and Jess were all right, then pointed vigorously seaward to the black thing they were trying to reach.

As one, the group on the dock responded by turning to peer in that direction. Soon catching sight of the spot of black, they hurried toward the end of the pier for a better view. By this time the squall had slackened.

Heads down against the wind, Don and Jess pushed on, climbing log over log until Don, in the lead, began hearing creaking noises and feeling movement beneath him. He knew he was now over water. To keep his balance, he spread his arms and legs wide and rode the swell. Scowling into the drizzle, he studied the debris ahead. A minute later, when he shouted back over his shoulder, his voice rang. "Jess! Right over here. It's a big black Angus!"

Speechless with wonder, the fishermen scrambled over several logs and onto a great tangle of underbrush and trees.

It gave because of floating in the bay, but it didn't sink more than a few inches deeper into the water. Rather, it seemed remarkably stout and strong. Manzanita bushes, willows and alders, most of their foliage gone, appeared to be tightly interwoven with the limbs of a tremendous pepperwood, forming a kind of bedding. Into that were laced two madrones and some young firs. Around the perimeter of the strange natural raft, redwoods of various sizes acted as floats. In the center of it all hung the Angus —limp, utterly exhausted, more dead than alive.

Yet he had seen the men coming. As they clambered upon his refuge, he tried to raise his head and even managed a hoarse bellow, although not a loud one. It sounded more like a throaty groan than anything else. His swollen tongue hung out the side of his mouth. He was so weak he could do nothing but lie helplessly across the crooked trunk of one of the madrones, his face in some manzanita leaves, his hoofs dangling down into the smelly water of the bay. Because the morning was early and cold, steam rose from his coat, matted with seaweed, salt, and grime.

Both Don and Jess stared in disbelief. That the steer could have been alive at all was one of those incredible miracles that neither man made an attempt to explain, for of the hundreds of cattle washed ashore along the Del Norte County coastline during the past few days, not one had been found to be breathing. Most were mangled and bloated carcasses, dead for a long time. All had to have been brought upcoast by longshore currents from the mouths of outfalling rivers. So, too, this one. There could be no question that the Pacific had carried him at least thirty miles, past towering cliffs and jagged offshore rocks.

"It just doesn't seem possible," Don Ford mumbled, reaching to touch the shaggy coat of the pitifully battered creature.

The men shook their heads sympathetically. They couldn't help trying to imagine how he had ridden this nest of brush and trees for three or four days through storm-tossed seas; how he must have soared to the crest of one mountainous wave after another, only to plunge down into the deep troughs between—and this in the mightiest gale to lash the Pacific Coast in a century!

"Tell me, Jess," Don said softly, "why isn't he crushed like all the rest? Whatever saved *this* one out of the hundreds and hundreds? Why *this* one?"

Jess's face was grave. He could think of no reply.

Don gave the salt-encrusted head a reassuring pat and then stood up. "Well, let's get cracking," he said. "We've got to pull the old fellow out somehow."

Jess threw him a startled glance. "How we ever gonna do that? He must weigh close to a ton."

The wind was blowing harder now. Don had to lean into it to stand at all, and the salt it contained was like ground glass, the way it stung bare skin. "We have to rig up something," he said, glancing around to see what he might have to work with.

"First off though, let's get help," Jess suggested, waving to their friends on the dock and the *Sea Belle.* "Hey, you!" he yelled. "Come on down. It's an Angus. *A black Angus.* Help us, you guys!"

The idea got through. All waved back that they understood, and some immediately began lowering themselves onto the debris.

Slowly, laboriously, they climbed over the vast jumble of giant trees that covered the Crescent City beaches and harbor. Several put themselves out of commission by falling through somewhere. The remaining few, picking their way more carefully, kept coming. But it was to be an hour before any of them stood on the incredible nest of brush that the steer had ridden into their log-packed bay.

Meanwhile, Don and Jess squatted beside the Angus, patting and talking to him quietly. The only indication that he was aware of their presence, however, was an occasional quiver when they touched him and a feeble attempt to see through the yellow matter that clouded his eyes.

Suddenly Don rose to his feet and grasped the end of a 2 x 12 plank that lay nearby. "Get hold of the other end, Jess," he said. "Set it down on that madrone over there, in the crotch of the big limb. That's right. Now, where's another'n?"

They found another milled plank sticking out between a screen door and an old rowboat. Together they pried it loose and laid it beside the first. A third and fourth, found floating, they placed alongside. They now had a sturdy ramp, well-anchored and pointed toward shore from a point close to the steer. Don looked down at it, a slow smile creeping up one side of his face. "Jess, if Slim and Bart can drag the *Belle* back to water this way, we ought to be able to get this poor critter back to land the same way."

Jess scanned the mass of debris they'd have to cross if they did. He shook his head dolefully. "Why couldn't I have been the lucky Klamath Glen guy marooned up there on the Ridge? Why, right now I'd be warming my toes before a roaring fire instead of . . . instead of . . ."

Glancing around at the flood victim, he gave a sharp cry. "Look, Don!" he exclaimed. "I believe he's dead."

Swiftly Don dropped into the brush and laid his fingers on the neck of the exhausted steer. For moments he crouched there, watching tensely, trying to find a pulse. The animal's eyes had rolled up and were staring into space, sightless and dull. His head had fallen back limply into the brushy matting; his jaw hung slack and out the side of his mouth a dirty brown froth oozed over his tongue, now so swollen that it almost filled his mouth. There was no visible movement of breathing.

Jess laid a hand on the grizzled face. "He's like ice. He's gone, all right."

"What a pity," Don muttered, looking down at the limp black form. "What can be right about this? He survives a terrible storm at sea and no telling what else— then he dies!" Don scowled and snatched a length of crabline he saw floating.

Sadly he and Jess turned to call to the first of the fishermen from the dock, who were just then dropping one by one onto the raft—the hulking giant who was Angelo; Krug, big, powerful, perspiring; young Kerry, arms and legs spread wide, steadying Rogers who was reeling in the wind. Amazement creased all their faces.

"Too late," Don told them. "The poor thing's died. Just now."

"*Died?*" Kerry exclaimed. "He isn't dead. Look!"

The two fishermen spun around to see the Angus raising his head slightly. But it was shaking so that he quickly dropped it back down among the glistening leaves and stems and heaved a long, quavering sigh.

"How about that!" Don shouted. "We thought he was gone."

Rogers' shoulders sagged. "Yet how could he possibly be alive?" he whispered hoarsely.

At that moment Slim and Bart from the *Sea Belle* eased themselves onto the bushes and stared in wonder.

"Gad! You have to see this to believe it!" Bart blurted.

Angelo nodded solemnly and crossed himself. When he spoke, his voice was soft and filled with awe. "See how he's completely surrounded by stuff that's protected him. Why, it's all around him. *All around him!*"

Kerry knelt and touched the big blocky head. "Seems like Someone meant for him to survive," he said.

Don stood up and, balancing himself on the floating mass, gazed shoreward. He said, "We'd better get him out of here fast or he won't make it."

"Just how?" Krug demanded. The others looked at Don in astonishment.

The big fisherman's voice was taut. "Lift him onto these planks and hope his legs'll hold him up."

Everyone turned to eye the plank ramp and to scan the two hundred feet or so of debris that lay between them and town. Slim and Bart grinned. They recognized their plan put to an unexpected use.

Unwilling to risk possible rebellion, Don cleared his throat noisily and went ahead in a firm voice. "Kerry, suppose you and Rogers take one of his front legs; Slim and Bart the other. Krug, would you and Angelo see if you can manage the hind quarters? Jess and I can work at his head and chest and try to keep him moving. This crabline I picked up will be great for a lead," he added, slipping the loop over the animal's head.

The men glanced sharply at one another but suppressed any question or comment. Each, muttering to himself, shifted around until he was at his assigned station, pausing only to brace and hold when a blow of salt spray hit full force.

The Angus moaned when Don, speaking softly, lay down beside him in the sopping manzanita. He moaned again when Don slipped an arm under his head and helped him roll over onto his sternum. This accomplished, he shook so with weakness that his head dropped heavily upon Don's shoulder. Worn out, he heaved a vast sigh, closed his eyes, and nuzzled against the fisherman's ear.

"Hey!" Bart called to the rest of the group. "Look at the critter now. Ain't that heart-rendin'?"

A smile flickered across Angelo's face. "Someone's treated this animal good. Doesn't seem afraid of us. Hope he's trusting enough that he'll let us handle him."

"You can say that again," said Krug, flexing his mighty arms.

Don let the steer rest awhile on his shoulder. Then he eased away so he could cradle the big head in the crook of his arm. It gave him an opportunity to scrutinize the thickening overcast. No question about it, the morning was growing darker and more menacing. Reflecting this, the sea had turned black. The smell of the air told Don that snow really was on the way. He frowned.

Noticing Kerry running a hand slowly along the back of the hapless steer, a thought crossed his mind. "Kerry," he called, "let's swap places. Take his head, will you? You like to be loved."

At this, the men laughed. They had often joshed the youth because all the animals in town seemed to follow him as if he were a Pied Piper. Good-natured about it now, as always, Kerry reddened but laughed with the others and edged over to the steer's head. Gently, he cradled it on his arm.

Don warned, "We've got to get going. Fast, too."

Every man looked up grimly.

"When we're ready, suppose I give the signal. Then together—somehow—*somehow* we hoist him up."

Jess pulled at the lobe of one ear thoughtfully. "I'm wondering if he's going to stand for all of that. You don't know farm animals like I do, Don. They spook awful easy, and if this one panics . . ."

"We've got to try."

The men lost no more time. Each made sure he was standing on something solid; each probed the shaggy coat in search of the firmest body grip and changed his position until he found one that offered the best possible leverage.

Don shouted into the wind, "Get a good hold, boys!"

While waiting for the rest of the crew to make last-minute adjustments, Kerry held the salt-encrusted head and spoke softly, trying to sound reassuring. Much to his surprise he saw that his voice got through. The steer's eyes opened and gazed up at him for a moment. Then they closed again and thick lashes spread onto his cheeks.

Don shortened the crabline. Carefully he eased a shoulder up into the great chest. His jaw muscle worked spasmodically.

"Everyone okay?" he shouted.

One by one the men indicated readiness.

"On the count of three, up we go," Don called. He waited a few seconds. "Take a deep breath."

A harbor buoy, rocking on the swell, tolled mournfully.

Don stiffened. His voice rose to a shout. "One—two—*three!*"

SIXTEEN

A Hoof
at a
Time

B oots now dug into bark and sent it flying. Knees strained against tree limbs. Burly shoulders hunched into flank and brisket. Big, rough hands, fingers spread wide, pushed upward. Teeth clenched and mouths contorted. Faces flushed with rush of blood.

The Angus did not panic or try to fight off his would-be rescuers. Instead, he was a mass of dead weight. Yet the eight fishermen, their muscles bulging and shuddering in sweating unison, slowly raised the huge steer until his hoofs came dripping out of the foul water of Crescent City's harbor; until finally they rested on the raft of trees and shrubs. Swaying precariously, the miserable animal appeared on the verge of collapse, but somehow his legs held him up.

"By gosh, he can stand!" Don whooped when he could get his breath. "We've got him up and he can stand!"

The lifting, however, had not been accomplished without incident. Several of the men tripped and sprawled over rain-slicked branches, and Jess slid partly into the water. Only Kerry had managed to keep his feet. Still hugging the steer's head to him, he was pleading softly, "Steady, fella. Steady there. We've got you now."

Don glanced around over the steaming body. "Check him good, boys," he called. "If anything's wrong, we better know right off."

Jess leaned into the chest and stooped to examine the front legs; Krug and Angelo the hindquarters. They found the hoofs broken and every joint swollen to twice its normal size, but, aside from this, the legs seemed to be sound enough. The animal showed nothing more than bruises and scrapes. A miracle, the men agreed as, with gentle hands, they went over the entire body.

Slim and Bart now spread out over the drift in search of more planks. Soon they had an extension of the walkway laid and had taken their places beside the wobbly steer. With support he was still able to stand, although unable to lift his legs.

"We're going to have to move each leg ourselves," Don shouted into the rain that was beginning to pound again. "And prop him up *too*," he added with extra emphasis.

So the men picked up his hoofs, one at a time, and set them down. With utmost care and strength they pushed and tugged to keep the big Angus upright and themselves from slipping and falling down through the tangle of debris. All the while Kerry held the big head and pulled forward gently. "Okay, fella, you're a-doin' fine. Just a bit farther now," he kept urging.

Gradually the Angus was eased from the brush to the planks.

The rescue party had a long way to go. They would be needing more solid bridging materials. When, at last, they all stood safely on the planks, Slim and Bart resumed their search for usable pieces and set them "end on" to the others. The rest of the men stood where they were, propping the steer with their bodies lest he topple, Kerry wiping out his eyes and squeezing rainwater into his mouth from a wet handkerchief.

All at once the swell under the debris gave a mighty heave, nearly hurling them all down. Only by plastering themselves tightly against the animal and holding firm did the men keep him on his feet. In this way they managed to ride out the jolt with its awesome crunching and grinding. But it had been a real brush with disaster.

Don glanced apprehensively toward the bay, then down through some crisscrossed logs at the troubled water below. "Tide's coming in," he panted. "Got to hurry this thing up."

He didn't have to warn that the flooding tide would soon shuffle and jam together everything under and around them—even the largest of the logs and redwood trees. The men nodded grimly and set to work with feverish determination. Strong, kindly hands again picked up and placed, one by one, the Angus's broken hoofs until the steer had plodded over the next several sections of platform. Not until a more solid feel underfoot told the fishermen they were at last over land did they dare stop to rest.

The makeshift walkway stretched ahead with agonizing slowness. Surfaces had become so shiny-slick that someone was always falling. Twice the steer went down, scattering planks and pitching some of his rescuers out into the jumble. The noise and commotion frightened him. Despite his swollen tongue, he bawled. Each time after he was helped to his feet, he had to be moved bodily.

Although long conditioned to a rugged seafaring life, the men began to tire. Don could see it in the way they drew close against the steer, hanging their heads and trying to regain their breath. "Rest all you can," he called, wiping the sweat and rain off his face with an arm.

"Can't let go," Jess panted. "He'll keel over for sure if we do."

Almost as if he had heard and felt he must redeem himself, the Angus tried to raise his head enough to nuzzle Kerry. It was then that the youth noticed a mound of salt-whitened curls piled on his forehead. At the same time he found himself gazing into a pair of liquid brown eyes. Something in them stirred him deeply. After a moment he was nudged backwards as the animal, unaided this time, pushed a front hoof forward a few inches and slowly shifted his weight onto it.

The effect was electric. A shout went up.

"How you like that?" Jess burst out.

"Did it by himself," Don called with a weary grin.

Krug jerked off his sou'wester and flung it into the wind. He stood bare-skinned and wet down to his wide leather belt. His massive shoulders and chest glistened. "Great stuff!" he cried. "Okay, boys, let's get on with it."

There was no need of planks for the next stretch of footing. The trunk fragment of a giant redwood offered an unbroken pathway through the drift for more than sixty feet. But it tilted upward just enough to exhaust both man and beast. Before they could plod its length the Angus was staggering and weaving.

Haggard faces turned toward the upper end of the drift and beyond to the sandy marsh and the rooftops of town. Three harrowing hours had passed since the steer had been lifted out of the harbor.

Angelo patted the black rump and fought for breath. "Almost . . . almost there," he gasped. His voice came out as little more than a whisper. No one could have heard him anyway: the rain still pounded endlessly, whipped into stinging fury by the gale. Slim and Bart, stomping into place a section of barn door and shoring it up, could scarcely see what they were doing. And ever present was the threat that somewhere along the line a part of the barn door might give way under the load it must bear—or simply fall apart.

"Ready with that?" Don called. He scarcely recognized his own voice.

Bart shouted back. "Yep, but watch it. Sure a long way down right in here. A good place to break your neck!"

Again everyone pulled himself together for the struggle. Strength was waning—they all knew it. To make matters worse, the Angus's every breath was now a groan, and he stumbled painfully with each hesitant step. Kerry took the great battered head in his hands and began to back cautiously, all the while coaxing and encouraging. The others strained and shoved and guided as best they could.

For another hour, superhuman will moved the steer over the jumble covering the beach to a madrone that lay athwart their path. This there would be no going around.

The men sagged. Their fatigue had become an aching monster that bedeviled every bone, every muscle and sinew. The wretched Angus, his sides heaving, seemed about to drop. Hoping to forestall such a calamity, Kerry held his head and talked to him quietly, as to a beloved pet. The steer tried to nuzzle again, but could no longer summon that much effort. The brown eyes looked up for a moment, then closed out of exhaustion too terrible to be endured.

In a fog of weariness, Don gazed back over the vast field of debris across which they had been dragging themselves all morning. Then he studied the edge of it just ahead. Now that they were almost there, how were they ever going to climb across the madrone trunk and work their way down through the jackstrawed trees and logs to the sandy marsh perhaps thirty feet below?

At that moment Slim and Bart came puffing back from a short scouting expedition. Slim pointed to a gap in the pile-up. "There's a spot yonder where we can angle down into the sand," he said.

Don spoke earnestly. "Ramp has to be gradual, you know. Not steep."

"Nope. Right. It won't be. We can get him out there," Slim declared confidently.

Don glanced around the group. Everyone nodded except Kerry. He was too busy to have heard. The Angus, eyes closed and head resting on the youth's hands, was trying to lick in some of the rain, now slacking to a drizzle. At the same time Kerry was scratching among the curls bunched on the broad forehead and rubbing back over the ears and down behind the jaw. He must have had a touch of magic in his fingers because the steer began to voice soft grunts of pleasure.

Don's tone was decisive. "All right, we build the ramp," he told Slim and Bart. "I'll help."

Turning to the others, he cautioned, "You guys hang onto him. Kerry—" a smile flickered across his face— "stay . . . stay just as you are. Okay?"

Again Kerry did not hear. The Angus was nuzzling his neck and blowing warm gusts noisily into his ear. Kerry reared back. A kind of amazed gladness washed over his face as he studied the battered black head, the dark eyes now trying to focus on him, their thick lashes sweeping over them. And when the pathetic animal heaved another of his vast and tremulous sighs, Kerry glanced around to make sure no one was looking. Then, grinning broadly, he encircled the shaggy neck with his arms.

Don and the others searched and labored for almost two hours before they were able to construct a usable ramp from the top of the drift down into the sand, and make it solid enough to support the huge animal and eight men. Eventually it was ready. The moment had come to move the steer over the madrone.

Only a medium-sized tree, the madrone nevertheless seemed to the sweating fishermen like a Mt. Everest of an obstacle. Yet somehow, a little at a time, they managed to pull the steer over it.

No sooner were all of them safely on the other side than the Angus collapsed. And when he went down, he took every man with him.

For a while they all lay panting. Kerry, the first to drag himself to his hands and knees, lifted the big black head gently onto his lap. Completely oblivious of the others, just then clambering stiffly and painfully to their feet, he began to plead with the exhausted steer. His voice was low and calm, but urgent. "C'mon, old fella. Aw, c'mon now. We're almost there. Don't conk out now, boy. *Not now!*"

Kerry was starting to draw the head closer to him when, on sudden impulse, he looked up and saw the men watching. Embarrassment caught at him. "Well!" he cried, his face reddening. "He don't have to lay down and die *now*. He don't have to fall to pieces just as we—"

Don interrupted quietly. "Okay, son, never mind. He's all right."

The Angus had begun to move. Slowly he rolled his eyes and gazed up at the fishermen clustered around him.

Once more they pulled him up. Once more he stood tottering uncertainly, braced on all sides by what was left of incredible will power and human strength.

By now none of the men could speak. Sweat soaked their shirts and dripped off their faces and mingled with the rainwater on the rough lumber at their feet.

They turned their backs to the sea and, protecting their faces behind hunched shoulders, huddled while a gust of salt-laden wind roared in and struck them full blast. Then wearily they guided the tottering Angus down the ramp they had prepared; down through the dim light in the depths of the driftwood—and miraculously out onto Crescent City's beach.

When they finally made it, only the steer remained on his feet. The rest of them, their faces expressionless, crumpled onto the sand and lay there as if they would never get up again.

SEVENTEEN

The Open Door

Not until that moment had any of the fishermen really appreciated the earth for what it is. They had always taken it for granted as something inherited by simple right of birth on the planet. It had been merely dirt and rocks and sand; something to be washed off and swept out; something to be dug and blasted. But not *this* stormy morning—or ever again in all their lives.

One by one the men dragged themselves up onto their knees and finally to their feet on the soggy ground. And there they stood, gaunt, hollow-eyed, a hundred years older; every muscle seeming to creak like the debris overhead.

Krug scanned the sandy marsh, studded with beaver grass, bull pines, and willows that stretched between them and town. "Now what!" he moaned in a gruff whisper.

No one answered. So benumbed was each of them that a thought beyond the moment was out of the question.

Presently Kerry called from where he was gentling the steer. "Don, look. The old boy needs water bad."

The Angus had raised his head enough to lick in dripwater streaming off a big redwood log in the maze above.

Don nodded wearily. "You know it. Poor fellow. Salt water's probably been pouring into him for days. We've got to find some fresh pronto."

A shout went up from a clump of willows nearby. It was Krug. "Look what we've got here!" he boomed. "A pond!"

The rain had filled a small depression among the dunes. The Angus had already smelled it, for he was sniffing in that direction. Thirsting mightily, he lowed. Then, slowly and painfully, the swollen legs responded to his need. He stumbled toward the pond, Kerry and the others helping.

Once he had plunged his face into the fresh water, he drank as well as his enlarged tongue would permit. He didn't drink his fill because Kerry wisely restrained him. But he did slake his thirst, snorted water out of his heavily encrusted nostrils, and let it wash his eyes.

"Best to let him drink some," Don said. "He's going to have the scours anyhow. It'll flush him out."

Krug stood with feet spread and arms folded across his chest. Kerry squatted beside the steer, stroking his flank, his expression one of deep concern. Absent-mindedly he passed a hand across his face. "I sure do wish we could truck him out of here," he said to no one in particular.

Angelo's reply was sympathetic. "Well, we can't—as you realize."

"No."

Slim, who had been eying Don, correctly read his thoughts. He tried to grin. "We walk him out. Right?"

Don grimaced wryly and rubbed his mustache. "That's about it." He looked relieved that someone had said it for him.

Jess inclined his head toward the hundred feet or so of sandy marsh yet to be crossed. "You got the gear shed in mind?"

"Yup, I have. We can build a fire in the woodstove and bed him down there."

"Yeah—*if* we can walk him to it." Jess's tone was skeptical.

"We not only can, my Indian friend. We *have* to."

Kerry threw Don a tragic look. His words rushed out in a sudden flash of feeling. "We better hurry, Don. I think he's sick. We got to call a vet—and find his owner."

Don sighed heavily. "Find his owner? How? I don't believe he has a brand or scar on him."

Kerry persisted. "Anyone who thinks anything of a steer would brand him, wouldn't they? Surely . . ."

Angelo broke in, his head bobbing up and down, his eyes bright. "Don't make any mistake about it—someone thought a lot of *this* critter, brand or no brand."

Gingerly stretching a cramped leg muscle, Don glanced at the sky. "Well, better get with it. It's quite a hitch across the beach."

All groaned their weariness, but in spite of his aches Bart chuckled. "Have you forgotten, you lazy bums? Tonight's Christmas Eve. Don't you have things to do?"

Everyone shook his head as if to clear away cobwebs.

It was hard to believe; Christmas had been a long way from their thoughts.

Kerry stood up painfully and prepared to move on. As he bent over to adjust the crabline, the steer laid his head on the youth's shoulder.

"The old fellow's taken to you, Kerry," Rogers observed, laying a friendly hand on his back.

Kerry glanced up and grinned. He finished tightening the lead and smoothed the coarse wavy hair beneath it.

Don laughed heartily. "I can see the animal is going to get more attention than most people," he said.

Kerry kept scratching around the Angus's ears. He did not look up. "Sure do wonder who he belongs to," he mumbled.

"No telling about that, fella," Don said quickly, "but we're sure going to try and find out whose he is."

With Kerry pulling firmly on the lead and the others again supporting from either side, the big steer turned away from the pond. For a moment he swayed, and if the men hadn't thrown themselves against him he would have gone down. Then he took his first halting steps toward town.

And so began the final lap of the incredible rescue. Even though this stretch was uncluttered beach, the crossing turned out to be one continuous struggle. The great battered body seemed to creak. With each successive move the gaunt flanks heaved and the groans grew louder.

The men groaned too. Eyes glassy, mouths hanging open and breath coming hard, they plodded onward. Their boots crunched deep in the wet sand. In pooling what re-

mained of their own waning strength, the eight fishermen wrestled the steer slowly, for they could see he was
steadily weakening. Yet none of them was willing to
accept the possibility that so valiant a heart might give
out before they could reach the gear shed, not fifty feet
away. Together they pulled and tugged and coaxed, step
after agonized step. Once, the Angus tried to lick Kerry's
hands, then gave up and simply let his head rest on the
youth's arm. And when he could no longer even hold his
eyes open, he stumbled along blindly.

A dozen yards from the gear shed, he fell.

Instantly the men knelt beside him, placing kindly
hands on his rough coat. Kerry dropped into the sand
and began to stroke his neck.

"He's alive," Don said presently, "but so help me, I
don't know why."

Kerry's eyes widened as he raised them to the fishermen.
"If we could just get him up once more. *Once more!*
We're so close."

Don glanced at each man in turn. "I'm going ahead
to open the shed and call Doc Stone," he said. "Keep
working on him."

Krug shook his head. "No use. That's *it* for him."

Kerry retorted through tightly clenched teeth, his voice
strong and clear. *"Oh no it isn't!"*

Quickly, but more gently than ever before, he lifted the
Angus's head onto his lap. The fishermen stared, feeling
helpless, defeated. Kerry leaned over and rubbed his
cheek back and forth across the pile of scraggly bangs.
Then, speaking softly, he sat back on his heels.

At last the steer's eyes opened. They were glazed and dim, but gradually, with a kind of benumbed fascination, they focused on Kerry's moving lips.

Kerry brightened. His voice grew animated. "C'mon, baby," he exhorted. "C'mon now. See that old shed? Inside a there you can lay and rest as long as you want— and sleep—and eat. And it's gonna be dry and warm and there'll be nowheres to go any more. We're gonna take care of you. I'll . . ." Kerry went on and on.

The dull eyes gazed up at him for a few minutes, then moved toward the open door of the shed looming in the mists. Almost imperceptibly a faint glimmer of light began to give them life. Whatever it was they saw appeared to be calling forth a last shred of will to live. Of his own accord, he raised his head and tried to bawl. He struggled to rise, too. With a sudden lurch the bony hips hoisted themselves, only to fall back. The body seemed incapable of carrying the brave spirit any further.

The fishermen moved fast. In time they had the steer back on his feet.

After that there was no stopping him. Somehow he was able to respond to Kerry's urging. Weaving an uncertain course on stiff legs that wobbled, grunting and groaning every step of the way, he plodded toward the dark opening in the building ahead.

When the men helped him stumble through the doorway into the dry interior, there was little doubt among them that he knew exactly what a shed was for.

EIGHTEEN

End of the Line— Almost

Just as Don completed his call to the veterinarian's office, he heard hoofs clacking on the cement floor. Glancing up in surprise, he saw the steer, supported on all sides by sweating fishermen.

"Take him over in the corner by the stove and build a fire!" he shouted. "And shut the door, will you, Krug? We've got to make sure there's no draft in here. I'll order hay and straw and stuff from the feed store and try again to get Doc." With that he turned back to his desk.

The shellfish company used the big shed for repair work and storage of assorted commercial fishing gear. In it, stacked about, were crab crates and fish boxes as well as hundreds of cork floats and great piles of nets. Because the building was tight, it soon warmed after the fire in the woodstove began to roar.

Outside, a light snow was already falling. By night it

would cover the harbor and beach debris and all the redwood forest with a coat of glistening white.

The fishermen set to work on the Angus at once, wiping away the worst of the salt and grime, hurrying to ready him for his straw before he should collapse again; gentling him all the while.

Jess was pulling some heavy nets back against the wall when the feed store truck arrived. Quickly the men carried the heavy bales inside and piled them a short distance from the stove. Within minutes, some of them had cut the binding wire and were spreading and fluffing the straw. The bales of grass hay and a hundred-pound sack of Steer Fat they placed nearby.

All this time, Kerry remained with the steer, wiping him off, giving him a small drink, scratching around his ears, talking softly—trying to keep him on his feet until all was prepared.

Don had just completed another call to the veterinarian when he remembered an old blanket someone had tossed into his office closet. He grabbed it and strode to the men clustered around the Angus. "We can warm this at the stove and cover him," he said, handing it to Slim and Krug.

"We got to be sure and keep him warm and dry," Krug said significantly.

"If this critter don't get pneumonia, I'll be gaffed," Jess said darkly. "Where *is* Doc Stone anyhow?"

Don rubbed his mustache. "Gone to Smith River. Some sick cows at Tidewater Ranch. He could get flooded in there, considering how things are."

Kerry threw the tottering steer a tragic look. "Oh, *no,*" he breathed.

Don hurriedly reassured him. "Doc will be calling in pretty soon. One way or another we'll hear from him."

"We've got to," Kerry said in a tight voice.

Rogers tossed the drying-rag over his shoulder. "We better bed this animal fast. He's about to cave in. If he does, we'll never get him up again."

Kerry moved to turn him. Assisted by every man, the Angus stumbled the last half dozen steps of his long journey. Once he stood on the thick bed of straw, and as if he realized he had finally reached the end of the line and could give in to his exhaustion, his legs buckled. He went down ponderously. With a hoarse groan that seemed to well up from the depths of him and embody the tortures of all ages past, he rolled over, shuddered, and lay still.

Never taking his eyes from the inert animal, Kerry grasped the warmed blanket Slim held out to him and swiftly spread it. On his hands and knees, he tucked the edges in snugly around the big black body. Then he stretched out beside the Angus and began comforting him. No one heard what he said, but they all saw the anxiety on his face.

Suddenly the steer gulped in a deep breath, let it go in a tremendous sigh, and sank into unconsciousness. When he did, Kerry allowed his own fatigue to take over. Unable to move or worry any more, he covered his face with his arms. Gradually he relaxed until he, too, was breathing regularly.

The men watched for a few moments, then dragged themselves stiffly to the stove and dropped into the chairs there.

Slim and Bart slumped and let their heads fall forward, appearing to doze. The rest either tested aching muscles or leaned elbows on thighs and ran shaking hands over their faces and through their hair. For every one of them, this was a moment crammed with realization of what they had been through that day. In the quiet of the shed and the warmth radiating from the stove, there was nothing to distract them from their own throbbing pains. Countless black-and-blue marks, unnoticed before, now felt too sore to touch. Raw hands burned, blisters broke. The men paid little attention when the telephone rang and Don hurried into his office.

Eyes heavy-lidded with weariness, they did look up when he rejoined them. "That's that," he said. He had the air of a man not only worn out but depressed as well. The big fisherman glanced at the sleeping youth and lowered his voice. "Sure enough—Doc can't come. Can't get back from Smith River. Rising water's cut him off."

Everyone exchanged glances.

"Then everything's up to us," Angelo whispered.

Don laughed shortly and, backing up to the stove, began to rub his thighs. "Doc didn't want to believe me when I told about . . . him. He said nothing—*nothing* —could have lived in such seas as we've been having. He said the Coast Guard guys told him waves have been over thirty feet high out there. Said the steer'd have been brained right away quick. And as for surviving among all those big redwoods grinding around out in the harbor— well, he just haw-hawed."

Slim scratched his head in amusement. "I bet he couldn't

believe you either when you told him the old boy doesn't have a broken bone in his body."

"I'll say he couldn't—or that he came to us in a tidy nest of small stuff that was all around him protecting him. What's more, I got the funny feeling he thought I'd gone storm-crazy or sumpthin'," Don snorted. "Anyhow, we aren't going to have a vet."

"I hope Doc told you what to do," Rogers said. He was watching the steer, whose breathing was becoming more and more labored.

Don stretched cautiously and hooked his thumbs in his belt. "Yup, he did, Rogers. He told us to keep him warm, flush him out with all the water he'll take for a day or so, and, like I said, expect the scours."

"And pneumonia?"

Don cleared his throat. "And pneumonia."

The men frowned.

Don knew well how, during those harrowing hours behind them, they had all grown fond of their Angus. Something about him had touched their hearts—the softness of his eyes perhaps, or whatever it was that made him want to nuzzle and lay his head on Kerry's shoulder. In a tired voice Angelo spoke of this, remarking again how he acted like some animal that had been used to people; one somebody had cared for and loved.

Bart agreed. "Yeah, I was thinking the same thing. Otherwise he'd have panicked and fought rescue like the very devil."

Don's voice came out strong. "You can say that again. And if he had struggled out there, it would have been just too bad."

He massaged a bruised back muscle and wondered how they had ever managed to save the incredible steer. At length he said: "Some of us will have to stay with the old fellow. We can't leave him alone."

Before anyone else could answer, Angelo volunteered. "Fine for me tonight or tomorrow, whichever you'd rather."

"Tomorrow, my friend, is Christmas," Don reminded him. "You stay home with that wife and dozen kids, y'hear? After tomorrow . . ." Don spread his hands.

Krug had risen and moved closer to the stove. "Why don't we go it in pairs?" he suggested.

Don inclined his head and with a question in his eyes looked at each man in turn. All nodded their willingness.

Jess got up painfully and went over to the straw. For a few minutes he stood listening to the animal's breathing, which had grown raspy and fitful. The Indian scowled and ambled back to the stove. "You and me tonight?" he asked Don.

"That's what I kind of had in mind."

"Slim and I can take over in the morning," Bart put in after a conference with his brother.

Angelo looked across the stove at Krug and received a nod to his implied question. "Okay for us tomorrow night," he said.

"I'll go it with the kid," Rogers said, indicating the sleeping Kerry.

Don smiled his relief. "Good. We'll work this thing out. Can't get at the boats for quite a spell anyhow."

Since most of the men were now fairly warm and dry and anxious to go home, they got up one by one and be-

gan to test their stiff muscles. Each moved as if over-
taken by old age. The terrible ordeal they had shared had
left its mark.

Slowly they dragged themselves toward the pile of
straw. There they stood for a time, gazing down upon their
steer. Because of the blanket, only his head was visible,
the mouth hanging open so he could breathe. Don's eyes
swept quizzically over the faces of his men. He saw their
reluctance to leave and sensed their fear that after they
had gone, the steer would weaken and slip away. He
knew exactly how they felt. There was just something
about that big Angus . . .

Presently the men turned away. Buttoning up their
shirts and jackets, they shuffled to the door and opened
it a crack.

The wind had died to an occasional whine but snow
was falling more heavily. Slim turned to grin. "Merry
white Christmas," he called in a whisper. With sudden
resolve, the brothers hunched themselves and stepped out
into the cold. The others followed.

After the door had closed, Don dragged slowly back
to the stove, where Jess sat, head on hands. "Know something, Jess?" he said, making an effort to speak quietly.
"It's almost five o'clock."

Jess raised his face. "It is? I'd forgotten about time.
Never thought about it, somehow."

"Me either."

"And it's Christmas Eve?"

Don nodded. "It sure enough is." He reflected a moment, his hands jammed deep into his jeans pockets.

"What a Christmas for the folks along the rivers. What a nightmare!"

"No one in the Redwood Empire will ever forget this'n," Jess muttered, then settled back in his chair and closed his eyes.

Don sauntered to the window and looked out toward town. For a time he stood watching the neon lights flicker on, one here, one there, in the early darkness of December. Through the snowflakes they glowed brilliantly.

Too tired to move, the big fisherman rested his arms on the sill and listened as the carillon bells of the church tower began to peal the season's tidings: "Joy to the world. . . ." For a few minutes he lost himself in the comfort of peace and beauty. The little community had never seemed dearer to him.

When the music stopped, Don sauntered back to the stove. "Jess," he whispered, "I believe I remember something about a cup of coffee."

The Indian roused and yawned. "Was that this morning?"

"Sure was. Just this morning. I'll go put on the pot."

But he didn't. Not right away. Instead, he and Jess walked over to the steer.

Instantly they saw that his breathing had become shallow and difficult. Squatting on his haunches, Don laid his fingertips on the animal's nose. It was hot and dry. Jess's eyes bored into Don's. Don pulled the blanket back far enough that they could smooth the shaggy hair. The Angus did not stir.

Nor did Kerry, whose hand rested limply on the steer's shoulder.

NINETEEN

Crisis

Later in the evening the winds howled in again and whipped wildly through the redwood forests, the same as they had the day before and the day before that.

The black Angus stirred restlessly and often raised his head to listen. When he heard the shrill whistling under the eaves, fear welled up within him—fear and no doubt frightful memories. Mixed up with the wind was the roar of angry waves tumbling him over and over; the terror of being hurled against logs and stumps and whole redwood giants; the crush of dark watery walls of water poised overhead, then plunging down upon him. Groaning in his dreams, the animal twitched and shook until at last his horrors were soothed away by kindly voices and gentle hands.

Hours passed; the night wore on. In that time different hands tended him, sponging his feverish nose, cooling his mouth with a little water. Yet there were two hands whose touch soothed and quieted him more than any of the others.

Kerry sat with the steer continuously. "There's no place I got to be," he told Don and Jess. "Anyhow, I like this straw. It smells good and it's warm in here."

Don squatted in the straw nearby and occasionally stole a glance at the youth. Kerry had appeared on the dock one day and applied for work. The men really knew nothing about him except that he was a drifter. More often than not he had reported to the job with a stray mutt trailing at his heels. Don was curious.

"Ever have a pet of your own?" he asked at length.

Kerry shook his head. "Me? No. Places like I been— orphanages, foster home—didn't have money for kids and animals both. So I've just kind of had lots of pets wherever I go. All over the country." He shrugged aside further questions.

When finally the Angus awoke, a drab Christmas morning had tinted the frost on the windowpanes with a pale gloom. No doubt everything around him blurred into shapeless forms and shadows, but he seemed to hear voices speaking in subdued tones. His trembling head turned toward them—and found a shoulder to rest upon. As two arms went around his neck, he gave a plaintive sigh. Then, because he was still too weak to hold himself up any longer, he let the gentle hands help him lie back down.

All Christmas Day his condition worsened.

Late in the afternoon the shed door burst open. Krug and Angelo staggered in, literally blown in by the wind.

"Merry Christmas, you guys!" Angelo called, his smile

radiating holiday good will. Then he sobered and, with Krug beside him, stood gazing at the black steer lying inert in the straw. He spoke haltingly. "He isn't . . . isn't . . ."

Kerry looked up, his face drawn. "No, he isn't, Mr. Angelo," he said gravely. "But he's most awful sick."

The steer's fever was soaring, for that morning pneumonia had taken hold. He coughed almost constantly, a harsh dry cough at first, then the low moist kind as the sickness progressed.

Before dark his eyes glazed over and he was breathing heavily through his mouth. He could be heard clear across the shed, and no one had to listen at his chest to detect the rattle inside. Without medical aid, the fishermen could do little but stand by and watch the animal's strength ebb, hour after hour.

Kerry hovered over the wretched Angus as tenderly as a mother over a sick child. Keeping vigil with him were various ones of the fishermen and their families as they could get there. Someone was always near to help Kerry keep the steer's nostrils moist and bathe the bleary eyes gazing up at them so full of trust. Others moved about, cleaning up after him and putting down fresh straw. Once, while the men were talking together, they agreed that although sympathy and care were due any living thing so disabled, this suffering barnyard critter was somehow wringing them all out. Yet no one could say exactly how or why. He just did.

By now many townsfolk had heard about the big Angus that had washed into the harbor and been rescued by their commercial fishermen. Almost immediately reporters began to write what they thought to be his story. Because none of them had the slightest idea where he had come from or to whom he belonged, they did a lot of supposing. Even the radio and television stations, picking up the news, kept speculating on how he had managed to live long enough to be swept into the bay; and, having been brought to safety, whether he would survive after all.

"*Something* saved him," people insisted. "He *has* to live."

But this seemed far from a certainty.

"What a fantastic animal!" the evening newscaster exclaimed with awe, and, wishing to honor anything so incredibly durable and heroic, named him Captain Courageous. After that, more and more townspeople flocked to the gear shed. Most dropped in out of curiosity, one or two because they thought he might be theirs.

With dismay they learned that his sickness was critical; that the new crisis he faced could easily be his last.

Far into Christmas night the steer's temperature and rate of respiration climbed steadily. All the men who had rescued him now gathered to help him fight for his life. They kept blankets tucked in around his tortured body and patted him sympathetically. In countless ways they tried to let him know they were there, trying to help.

About two o'clock in the morning the crisis came.

Beside him during those fateful hours sat Kerry and Rogers. The others lingered nearby, watching, concern clouding their weather-beaten faces. The steer's tongue hung out the side of his mouth, and over it bubbled an ugly froth. His breathing labored until it appeared he could no longer pull oxygen into his congested lungs. Every gasp brought a gurgle in his throat.

In a welter of dread, Kerry dabbed a wet cloth at the parched nose and watched the worsening grow. Once he cried out at the wind whining around the corners of the building. "Why can't that racket stop! It's got to. If it don't it'll finish him for sure!"

Rogers' voice was husky but calm. "Steady, boy. He don't hear it. He can't."

Kerry sagged dejectedly. "No . . . I guess not," he murmured.

A surge of desperation seized him. "But he's got to have quiet. He's so sick. He's . . ."

Suddenly the whole body stiffened. The legs strained and stretched full length; the neck pulled the great head back as far as it could go, and the mouth jerked wide open. The steer was fighting for air. The end appeared to be near.

Kerry bent over him. His jaw tightened. He struggled mightily with himself until, uttering a cry of despair, he threw himself down in the straw beside the Angus and let his misery go. It burst forth like the breaking of a dam.

"He's gone through so awful much," he sobbed. "And he's so kind of . . . special. Dear God, You must have meant for him to live. Please—*please* don't let him die!"

Rogers said nothing. He merely took hold of the youth's shoulder. Wisely, he and the others knew that all they could offer was silent strength.

Then, just as suddenly as the huge animal had stiffened, he went completely limp. There was no movement of any kind, no sign of life. Glancing sharply at one another and Kerry, the fishermen clustered together and awaited the last breath the steer would ever draw.

What seemed to be an eternity passed. The Angus gave a shallow gasp. It was slightly longer than the breath before it; the next one he drew was a bit longer than that.

Swiftly, Kerry sponged out his open mouth. The tongue rolled the water around and licked out for more. Something was different about the steer now. They all saw the change.

Don's brow furrowed thoughtfully. He placed his fingertips on the hot nose and held them there for a long time. When his eyes finally met Kerry's, they were bright. "Kerry," he said, "I believe his fever is breaking."

The youth nodded wordlessly, his face set, his lips drawn thin, as if he was determined to believe, no matter what. Slim and Bart looked on, spellbound. Very slowly the labored breathing began to lose some of its roughness and began to come with more ease and from greater depths.

During the anxious hours that Kerry watched the passing of the crisis, the tense lines in his face gradually relaxed until finally, out of relief too enormous for speech, he impulsively ran a hand through the bunch of curls on the steer's forehead. Then he slumped. He was spent.

The Angus may have remembered other hands that had gentled him just this way, because with considerable effort and for the first time since Christmas morning, he attempted to lift his head. Quite plainly his vision was unclear and muddled during those few shaky seconds; yet he appeared to glimpse the youth beside him. He tried to focus his eyes on Kerry but weakness quickly overtook him and his head sank back into the straw.

Kerry's breath caught in his throat. "You know, I think he's gonna be all right," he rasped in wonder. His voice rose. "I think he's gonna make it!" Up on his knees now, he grabbed Don's arm. This time he spoke firmly and positively. "Don, he's gonna make it!"

"I believe he is," Don agreed, voicing a note of hope.

Kerry swung around and shouted at Jess, at that moment warming one of the blankets at the stove. "Jess, come here and see. He's gettin' better!"

By then, Kerry, his face shining, had flopped down and was pleading with the steer. "C'mon, baby, keep fighting. Hang in there now and you'll be okay. When you're all well, we'll . . ."

The fishermen did not hear the rest of all he said. Bart's voice, deep and upbeat, commanded their attention. "You guys know something? This animal acts just like he was used to someone fussing over him. Now honest, don't he? Don't he take to it like a salmon to fresh water?"

"And you bet he knows Kerry from the rest of us," Rogers added with feeling.

Krug's cropped head wagged back and forth. "He's got a way with animals, that's for sure."

The men found themselves laughing as they remembered all of Kerry's dogs and cats they had treated to fish and bits of their lunches out on the company pier.

Kerry paid no attention to the conversation. He was still exhorting the steer, feeling the nose, listening at the chest.

To the fishermen there was little question now but that

the Angus was passing safely through the crisis and was on his way to recovery.

Once sure of this in his own mind, Kerry got to his feet and stood gazing pensively upon the animal, sleeping naturally at last. Weary from his long and constant vigil, he had no inclination for small talk, but he did smile when the others fell to discussing their patient's apparent indestructibility. It was a time of gladness for them all.

After a while Rogers spoke quietly to Kerry. "Thanks to you, he's going to pull out of this."

"He sure as heck is," the youth replied with a flash of exultation.

"Well then, while he rests, why don't you come home with me? We got an extra bedroom nobody's using. My wife's cooked up a turkey and fixin's. Lots more'n we can eat, the two of us. Christmas somehow . . . sort of got . . . delayed, but . . ."

Kerry's smile widened into a grin. Turning to Don and Jess, he thumped each of them joyfully and to the others made a round AOK sign with thumb and forefinger. Then, striding eagerly across the shed, he followed Rogers out into the dawn.

TWENTY

Not a Single Identifying Mark

From that night on, the steer showed steady improvement. After his temperature broke, his nose cooled and moistened and his eyes brightened. In three or four days his lungs had cleared remarkably and he was able to stand and move around.

About the same time, the heavy ground-level fog and clouds lifted from forest and sea, permitting helicopters to range far up the winding river valleys of the Smith, the Klamath, the Trinity, and the Eel. But the overcast still hung low enough that the pilots often got lost. For one thing, they could not locate the villages indicated on their maps, and small wonder—the little towns weren't there any more. All that could be seen were ribbons of thundering brown water cutting wide swaths through valleys of skyscraping redwoods. Nevertheless, the pilots continued their search for flood victims stranded atop houses and barns and on high ridges of land. These they picked up and brought to town. So, as the days passed, more and more people came to hear about the dramatic rescue of the black Angus from Crescent City's logged-in harbor. By the dozen they streamed in to see him.

At first they could only stare in amazement, as they might have gaped at an unidentified object from outer space. But their awe was soon replaced by warm feelings akin to the pleasure of visiting with an old friend. Invariably they found themselves patting Captain Courageous, even talking baby talk and returning with tidbits they thought he might relish.

"This beast is a bottomless pit!" one of them exclaimed, laughing. "I don't think he's ever going to stop eating."

While this appeared to be true enough, the Captain enjoyed the attention he received even more than the treats. With happy abandon he smeared his wet nose over all who came near, and sometimes followed them to the door when they went to leave. He couldn't have shown more plainly that he not only liked his visitors but wanted their indulgence as long as they were there. Every time the shed door opened, the steer would look up expectantly, his eyes alight. Before anyone actually became aware of it, he was thoroughly spoiled.

A woman mentioned this to Don one day while wiping off her face where the Angus had licked it. Don guffawed. "You're so right. But doesn't he spoil awful easy? More like he's been spoiled all his life."

After his picture appeared on the front page of the Crescent City *American* with the title "Captain Courageous" under it, people said he really turned on the charm.

A large group happened to be with him the morning

Kerry burst into the shed, waving a newspaper. As if pulled together by a drawstring, they clustered around to look at the photograph and read the account of his rescue.

"Show him his picture," a small boy begged, thumping the steer's flank. "It's him. He's got a right to see it."

Caught up in the tide of excitement, Kerry held the paper up in front of the Angus. "See, baby, this is you," he teased. "You made the front page. How about that!"

Everyone watched in amused silence, but no one claimed to be absolutely certain that a flicker of recognition appeared in the big brown eyes. Still, Captain Courageous did stop chewing his cud for a moment and gazed intently at the paper.

"You don't think he knows that's him?" Kerry shouted triumphantly. "Of course he does. What'd you expect him to do when he saw himself—jump straight up and moo?"

Hearty laughter broke out.

In the days that followed, the Captain sucked every finger he could get hold of—and finally the dress of any woman or girl who happened to be standing close by.

"Isn't that pretty juvenile?" a worldly-wise teen-ager simpered, trying to smooth out the damp wrinkles with her hands.

This brought out chuckles, for, as one of the girl's friends pointed out, "Cap" was a full-grown steer and rugged by any standards. His callers had to agree, however, that such a display of affection by a half-ton Angus made him a personality of some distinction. And most people referred to it as comical, the shed often ringing with laughter.

A man standing to one side, watching the fun, rubbed

a thumb back and forth across his chin. "Odd," he mused. "Somehow this steer reminds me of one our friends in Klamath Glen had. Couldn't be that'n, though."

"Why not?"

"You seen the Glen?"

"Not yet."

The man snorted and wagged his head dolefully. "Almost as clean as a ballroom floor."

As soon as the Captain was on his feet, the Brands Inspector dropped in and clipped the places where cattle are usually branded. But neither he nor the veterinarian, who had checked earlier, could find a mark of any description —not even a tattoo or evidence of an ear tag.

"Well, we'll never identify this one," he concluded at last, heaving a sigh of resignation.

"There ought to be some way," Kerry argued. "He has to belong somewhere."

"Figure it out for yourself," the inspector shot back. "What would a claimant be able to say? 'I've lost an Angus. No, he doesn't have a single mark on him. He's just black and two or three years old.' "

"I see what you mean," Don put in thoughtfully.

"You've a problem here. Sure as fate, more'n one fellow is going to try and establish ownership, just to get him. You'd better be finicky about identification, Ford, or somebody will grab this steer who has no right to him. I don't know how you're ever going to decide who he belongs to. It's a lead-pipe cinch—he can't speak up for himself and say, 'Hey, Mister, I'm yours—remember?' So there you are." The inspector shrugged and went about collecting his equipment.

For more than a week, assorted townspeople flocked to the gear shed and mingled with countless ranchers and dairymen. One of them, a beauty operator, laid skilled hands in the waves Kerry had set in the hair on the Captain's shoulders. "What I wouldn't give for a natural wave like this," she murmured enviously. "Where did you come from, Cap?"

She didn't receive an answer to her question. The steer was busily going over her hand with his rough tongue.

A group of Cub Scouts fared no better. They had to be content with patting him and having their faces licked in return and speculating as to his origin.

"Maybe he was a cow that lived in the ocean," one of the Cubs cried, and they all squealed with delight at the thought.

He might as well have lived in the ocean, because no one could find out anything about him.

Finally the rains stopped and the clouds scudded on inland, leaving the sun to bathe sodden redwood country in a golden glow that revived every living thing it touched.

Lumbermen from the Trinity, the Klamath, and the Eel then came to town and began looking for their own stamped logs and lumber so they could haul it back to their mills as soon as the condition of the roads and bridges would allow. They knew that whatever remained unclaimed would have to be burned where it lay. Huge fires were to blaze for weeks before the beaches would once again be clear of debris. An assist from the sea helped free the harbor itself: tides had brought it in; tides took it away.

With the return of good weather, Don and Kerry led the Angus out into the warmth of the sunshine. There, through the middle of the day, he nibbled some of the beach grasses, pausing only to note each new noise and smell; always watchful for visitors, who continued to arrive in greater numbers as the news of him spread.

Because it soon became evident that a commercial fishing gear storage area was no place for a big farm animal —not permanently, anyway—Don was often asked what he intended doing with the Captain. "I have no idea. I wish I did," he answered over and over. "We've grown pretty fond of the old boy. Hate to part with him. But none of us is a cattleman, and feed's expensive."

"This steer has to belong to somebody," Del Norte County residents kept insisting. And more than one added, "If he were mine, I sure would want him back."

Every day many searched over his body for small marks: a scar, perhaps; a misshapen joint, a kink in his tail. All had to concede that the animal wasn't theirs. What they sought was never in the right place or of the proper shape or size.

Contentedly, the Captain basked in all the attention. He also returned it with interest. A Ferndale cattleman, examining him for a small scar one of his own Angus had sustained from barbed wire, got his neck swiped by the Captain's rough tongue.

"Wow!" the man roared, backing off. "That's more lovin' than I get from my wife."

Everyone burst out laughing.

"Bet he'd follow you right into the house," someone suggested.

"Bet he would too. He loves everyone he sees."

"I'd sure like to have this critter," the cattleman said, wiping his neck with a handkerchief.

"But not to butcher!" a heavy voice protested.

"Of course not to butcher! He's more than earned the right to live. I'd want him because of what he's done." A wry smile pulled at the cattleman's mouth. "And because of the way . . . the way . . . he . . . *is*."

"You and everybody else," Kerry laughed.

Late the same afternoon, while he was brushing the Captain's coat for the second or third time that day, a girl clad in a black all-weather coat and hat knocked at the shed door. Don was about to leave but decided to wait when she smiled engagingly.

"I'm Gildee Griffin," she told him, stepping in out of the drifting fog. "I'm a freshman up at high school. I knew an Angus that belonged to a boy who lived in Klamath Glen. His father was a logger there."

"Maybe this is the one," Kerry offered hopefully.

The girl tucked back under her rainhat a strand of red hair the sea breeze had loosed. "To tell you the truth, I just sort of wanted to see the animal for myself," she admitted as if in apology. "Everyone's been talking about him. He couldn't possibly be the Klamath Glen steer, you know. That one wouldn't be alive. His family was washed out—home, barn, trees, everything. Their property is under ten feet of mud."

Don passed a hand over his mustache. "I'm sorry to hear that," he said.

Together they walked to the Captain, the girl silently

watching the steer munch selected wisps of hay; studying him intently from head to tail.

"He the one?" Kerry asked presently, drawing the brush down the animal's side with elaborate care.

She shook her head. "He can't possibly be. But even if he were, how could I tell? Don't they all look alike?"

Don was quick to respond. "No, not really. They're pretty much individuals, same as people. Especially an animal that's been hand-raised like some are."

"Even without any special marks or anything?"

"Most always, sure."

Unexpectedly, the Captain punched the visitor's hand with his wet nose when she wasn't looking. The coldness of it shocked her into bubbly laughter. She reached out and stroked his soft throat, which brought his head up. He regarded her from beneath sweeping lashes, his eyes awash with instant affection.

"You scamp," she rebuked with mock sternness. "I'm going to come back and steal you. You're an outrageous flirt." Her hand strayed up the steer's jawline and into the ringlets bunched loosely on his broad, hard forehead. He rolled his tongue out as if to draw her closer to him.

Don chuckled when he saw the pink deepening in her cheeks. Kerry, watching from the other side of the steer, had to laugh. "He nuzzles everyone," he said.

The girl glanced up at the two men, a quizzical expression creeping into her eyes. "Funny," she said. "*He* did that. The boy's pet."

Kerry laid the brush aside. "Hasn't the kid been in to see if the Captain's his?"

"No, he hasn't."

"How come?"

Gildee shrugged. "Everybody's tried to get him to come down here, but he won't. Nothing can budge him. Nothing."

Kerry threw her a look of surprise. "Why not?"

"Well, all he's done is hunt for his steer for days and days—ever since he and his folks got down off the Old Ridge Road. It was their camper that was stranded up there for so long. He's even been ditching school to look. He and his dad have combed the beaches and coves for miles both north and south of the mouth of the Klamath. They've looked everywhere. Everywhere he could possibly be. Of course, you know what they found." Gildee made a face. Her mouth trembled. "Dead animals everywhere."

"Even so, why . . ."

Gildee raised her eyebrows. "Can't you imagine what all those hundreds of rotting carcasses would do to him? He's had it. He's all shriveled up inside. Anyway, he knows this animal here can't possibly be his. Not thirty miles from where he washed into the sea! So why come down here and get torn up some more? You understand. It's real obvious what happened to his steer. I'm worried about him, Mr. Ford."

Don and Kerry caught the shine of tears in her eyes. They frowned and murmured their sympathy.

"Where is this kid?" Kerry asked at length.

"Out at Northcrest, staying with friends while his folks are down at the Glen trying to decide what to do. The mill's reopening soon."

Aloud, Don wished he knew what to suggest.

Kerry pursed his lips in thought. "Couldn't *you* get him to come down here, just on the outside chance that maybe this . . . this one . . . ?" He fumbled for words.

Gildee's eyes widened. Her voice rose. "Oh, I've been working on it—hard. But it's no use. No use, *period*. Brad just turns away from me every time I mention the subject. It's all that bad."

For a few moments there seemed to be nothing more to say. Kerry broke the silence. "The Captain's owner has to be somewhere," he said softly. "We ought to find him. Whoever he belongs to loved him very much."

Gildee cocked her head and gave Kerry a sidewise glance. "How do you know that?" Her puzzled gaze searched his face.

Kerry returned it with a look both gentle and understanding. "Animals, the same as people who are loved, show it," he said simply.

Gildee continued to study him as if such an idea had never before occurred to her. "They do?" she said.

Kerry nodded. "I think so."

The girl patted the Captain's neck once or twice and then ran her fingers through the curly bangs. As far as she was concerned, the matter was closed. "Well," she sighed, giving the steer a final pat, "I'd better get home. Mom will be waiting dinner." Then, smiling, she added, "Thanks for being so nice."

Reluctantly, Gildee turned away.

TWENTY-ONE

The Bunt
That Counted

Gildee's first step toward the door was a long one, taken head first, for quite unexpectedly there came a thump from behind, squarely where leverage provides the greatest thrust. Her rainhat flew off. Don and Kerry gasped as she stumbled forward, struggling to keep her feet.

Before she could sprawl, Gildee was able to recover herself. She whirled around to see the Captain contemplating her with what amounted to—in her own words later—"a wicked twinkle in his eyes."

Kerry hurried to pick up the rainhat and make sure the girl wasn't hurt. "You all right?" he asked.

Gildee nodded, never taking her eyes from the steer.

Don assured her earnestly, "Believe it or not, he meant that as a . . . a friendly gesture."

Gildee beamed. "I know he did."

Then, speaking straight to the Captain, she said, "Sweetheart, I told you I'd back away from you next time, and I didn't."

Don and Kerry glanced at each other in amazement. Don allowed the thought to enter his mind that these days even fine youngsters like this one sometimes acted strangely.

The girl did not wait for any inquiry into her mental health. Her manner was that of one who had arrived at a definite decision. "I wonder," she said to Kerry, "would you be willing to go talk to my . . . to this boy? Would you try to get him to come see the Captain?"

For a second or two Kerry was taken aback.

"Please?" she persisted.

Kerry shifted from one foot to the other uneasily. Caution slowed his reply. "What's the use? If he wouldn't come for *you,* I . . . I don't figure him coming for me," he countered.

Gildee appeared not to have heard his doubts. She went ahead eagerly. "Tomorrow morning sometime? It's Saturday. His folks will be returning from the Glen tonight. They should be with him when he comes down here."

Kerry could not find an answer immediately. Seeing his hesitation, the girl's eagerness subsided. Her tone became more urgent. "You'd know just what to say to him. You've got the same kind of . . . of caring for the Captain that Brad had for his steer. I know. I can tell." Her eyes probed Kerry's.

Then she added with some reluctance, "Of course, I have to be honest and say I'm almost positive he won't come."

"Then why . . ."

Gildee's voice carried a quickening spirit. "But it's worth a chance, isn't it? Even a slim chance? A *last* chance to find his pet? It is to me."

Kerry brightened. After a moment he nodded. "Then it is to me."

Don saw her to the door.

Saturday morning the shed hummed with activity. Not only did Captain Courageous have more company than usual, but all the fishermen except Kerry were there too, cleaning the shed, mending nets, stacking some new fish boxes. For the steer they laid fresh straw, filled his feed-box with grain and his tub with water—and they stopped often to pet him.

His soft brown eyes followed their every move.

Soon after ten o'clock, Krug, assisted by Slim and Bart, brought in a load of crabpots. This accomplished, the big German strolled over to the stove, scanning the shed to see who was there. "Where's Kerry?" he asked finally.

Rogers answered, for earlier he had given the youth the keys to his car and watched him drive away to North-crest. "Kerry's out hunting up some boy one of the high-school girls thought might know something about the Captain."

The fishermen worked along without comment for a while, bantering back and forth and calling greetings to visitors.

As the morning wore on, more people than ever moved in and out. Many of the men remained to gather around the woodstove and talk. Some of the women and children took flash pictures of the Captain with Christmas cameras or fed and patted him—and were abundantly rewarded.

Shortly after the town's noon whistle blew, Rogers sauntered restlessly to the door and peered out. Don joined him.

"Kerry must be having a tough time," Rogers remarked presently.

"The young lady said he would. I guess the boy's not about to go lookin' at more cattle. Can't say as I blame him."

"Either way, Kerry ought to be here pretty quick."

"Yup. Ought to."

Both men were starting to turn away when two cars pulled up nearby. The first one belonged to Rogers; in it were Kerry, an older man, and Gildee. The second was a red and white camper; in it a man, woman, and teen-age boy. The fishermen came alive.

"They're here!" Don shouted back into the shed. "I kind of believe Kerry persuaded the boy to come down after all. What do you know!"

The other fishermen went on with their chores. Most did not look up or even indicate that they had heard. The men had grown thoroughly skeptical of each new claimant.

As Kerry alighted from Rogers' car, he noticed the two standing in the shed doorway. Thrusting his hands into his jeans pockets, he hunched his shoulders and ambled toward them.

"Brad finally gave in and decided to come," he called in a matter-of-fact tone, a quiver in his voice betraying emotion of a different kind.

Rogers' usually sober countenance broke into an affectionate smile. Kerry frowned as he approached. He was tense and visibly shaken. "That's the hardest job *I* ever did," he said guardedly, his glance darting back to the others getting out of the camper. "A good Joe, this kid. He sure loved that steer that was washed away." He shook his head sadly. "I don't think much of dragging him down here like this. But Gildee—well . . ." He shrugged and spread his hands, then turned aside, his eyes suspiciously moist. "Darn! Brad deserves to have the Captain be his."

Rogers was sympathetic but, by nature, inclined to be realistic. "Easy does it," he cautioned. "The Captain can't be the one, you know."

Kerry set his lips.

"Remember," Don put in gently, "no matter what— you tried. You did what you could."

"If it only could have been enough," Kerry murmured, more to himself.

By this time the rest of the party had walked to the door.

Having to present strangers to one another was something Kerry obviously wasn't accustomed to doing. His introductions were awkward but the best he could manage. Afterwards, glancing around self-consciously, he wiped sweaty palms up and down his thighs.

The big logger and his wife, on either side of Brad, tried to smile their acknowledgments, but Don observed that they were as strung up as their tall blond son, just then wetting his lips with his tongue. Behind them hovered an older man, heavily browed, whom Don recognized as Brian Turner; at his side stood Gildee, her hands clasped tightly. All appeared distressed about Brad, his feet wide apart and standing too stiffly, his face gray and wooden, masking little of the dread that filled him.

Don stepped forward. "Mr. and Mrs. Hale—Brad—

I'm glad you're here about the Captain," he said courte-
ously. After his friendly eyes had swept the group, his interest was drawn to the companionable way the big
logger had placed an arm protectively around his son's
shoulders. He warmed at once. I know how he feels, he
thought. My boy's a manly kid too.

Monty's voice dropped low when he spoke. "We are
. . . we were . . . from Klamath Glen. Got wiped out
last month."

The fisherman expressed his regret and fell silent.

"We figured to take a look at your steer," the logger
went on. "My boy here had a pet Angus. He was much
—*very* much—loved. When the river cut across the
Glen, he . . ." He shrugged, glancing furtively at his son.
Then, in haste but with pride, he added, "We're going to
rebuild our house and barn, Brad and me, soon as spring
comes. Some of his school and 4-H pals have volunteered
to help. So if this steer should happen to be . . ." He
did not finish.

Don saw that the animal had been cherished, his dis-
appearance nothing less than a small disaster within a
big one. Such a wave of pity washed over him that he
tried to think how to soften the blow he felt to be in
store for the forlorn teen-ager. He brought his attention
back to the clean-cut boy, who was steeling himself to
stand tall and impassive when the moment came for him
to shake his head and turn away. Don was filled with ad-
miration.

"You want to see if this'n's yours?" he suggested gently.

Brad nodded. In bracing against one more heartbreak,
he lifted his chin defensively and hooked his thumbs
in the belt band of his jeans.

The big logger's brows drew together, "I've warned Brad that he oughtn't count on this animal being ours." His tone emphasized preparedness for certain disappointment. He faltered for an instant and cleared his throat, then went on: "You see, nothing at all—nothing—is left of our place. Your Angus can't very well be ours."

Jane interrupted to protest. "Now, Monty, we don't know this," she pointed out.

To Don and Rogers she said, "That's why we're here, Mr. Ford. Kerry told us Gildee thought your steer acted like—like . . ." Jane, too, seemed at a loss to express what she obviously wished so hard.

"Your animal have any identification marks on him?" Rogers asked Brad in a kindly voice.

Brad's shoulders sagged. "No sir. None." Swallowing hard, he turned to go.

Gildee blocked his path. "Brad—wait!" Her eyes flashed. She chose her words carefully. "Brad, *somebody's* steer, out of all the hundreds and hundreds, had *something* that saved him!"

Brad hesitated before her unexpected fire.

Kerry now stepped to the boy's side and, taking hold of his arm, slowly pulled him around. "Listen to me good, fella." His eyes bored into Brad's. "Wouldn't you always like to remember you did everything humanly possible to find that steer of yours? Wouldn't you say he had that coming?"

Brad flushed a dull red. "Well, yes. Sure," he replied, his voice strong.

"You can live with that," Kerry assured him. His tone softened. "We're going to have lumps all our lives, off and on. We got to expect 'em. That's how it is."

Brad's gaze flickered across the other's face just once. He was listening.

Kerry went on quietly. "You know as well as I do that the chances aren't good the Captain will turn out to be yours. With no marks on him, how you ever goin' to tell? But I bet you're man enough to get yourself the heck in there to see the only steer that did live through the flood—whether he's yours or not. He's a . . . a honey, I'm tellin' you. And I oughta know."

Kerry's voice broke. Embarrassed, he looked away. Determined to resist emotions that threatened to surface, he tapped Brad's shoulder with a fist. "Okay, let's go," he said lightly, as if the boy, not he, had made the decision. Then, glancing neither left nor right, he strode in through the open door.

Don sensed a new strength taking hold in Brad. It fascinated him. He could only stand back and stare at the teen-ager, who smiled crookedly at each of his parents and then, without a word, followed Kerry into the gear shed.

Brian Turner stepped in beside Rogers. "You can be proud of that Kerry lad of yours," he said sincerely.

Rogers did not correct him. "I am," he said.

Once indoors, the group paused to let their eyes adjust to the dim light.

"The Captain is entertaining his public," Kerry told Brad when they could see across the shed. "As usual, they're *all around him,* fussin' over him, spoilin' him rotten." He forced a laugh.

By now the visitors could see the crowd that surrounded the Captain and were watching him chomp blissfully on an apple a little girl had given him. Amused, Krug and Angelo, Slim, Bart, and Jess were looking on from the fringe and talking among themselves. Almost everyone else was laughing and remarking about the steer's spectacular appetite.

The Angus's big blocky head was in full view, framed between the orange sweaters of two high school lettermen. The newcomers could see him clearly.

All at once Brad gasped. Startled, Monty and Jane glanced at him and at each other.

Before they could say anything, Brad had snatched the knit cap off his head. For a few moments he was unable to utter a sound. Eyes wide, mouth hanging open, cap clutched in hand, he was pointing wildly at the Captain. A radiance lighted his face. He turned to his father and a hoarse half-whisper came tumbling out. "Dad—look! That's him! *That's him!*"

With a rush, long-pent-up grief exploded into happy tumult. Finding his voice at last, Brad shouted, and his joy rang throughout the shed. "Bahamas! *Bahamas! It's me, Bahamas!*"

The Captain heard. He stopped chewing. A gleam came into his eyes. He turned his great head toward the cluster of people just inside the shed door. When the remains of the apple dropped unnoticed from his mouth, all the gay chatter around him suddenly lapsed into the stillness of utter surprise.

An instant later, bawling loudly and tremulously, he broke through his ring of admirers, scattering them like redwood needles before the autumn winds. Then, claiming his loved one, he trotted across the shed to the sturdy blond boy who, fists clenched, arms outstretched, stood laughing as if his heart would burst.

Epilogue

Bahamas today is the picture of contentment and well-being. During most of the year, and along with others of his kind, less famous, he grazes flowered pastures high on the bluff above the mouth of the Klamath. Up there he can gaze out over the river and endless expanses of the Pacific. Weighing nearly a ton—considerably more than when the fishermen lifted him out of Crescent City's harbor—he looms larger lying down than his companions do standing up.

Of course no one ever thinks, much less speaks, of Bahamas in terms of roasts and steaks. The Klamath Chamber of Commerce has purchased him so that from here on out he may remain in his home neighborhood and live the life of a country squire. Every spring Bahamas is moved down to a grassy especially-built corral in Old Klamath Townsite, where all manner of goodies are bestowed upon him by friends, former neighbors, and summer tourists. So it is no surprise to anyone that he spoils as easily as he ever did. Quite obviously he simply picked up where he left off when the great flood of 1964 carried him away.

Meanwhile, for directing and leading his sensational rescue, Don Ford was feted at a banquet in Crescent City.

On that occasion a representative of the American Humane Society flew north to pay tribute by awarding Don a well-deserved medal of honor for compassion and bravery.

Many Glen folk have rebuilt, and a splendid new bridge, guarded at both ends by large golden bears, has replaced the old one. The demolished village of Klamath, however, had to be abandoned and another Klamath started where it would be safe from floodwater.

Travelers visiting Old Klamath Townsite can see Bahamas, and, if they like, do their bit to pamper him. Whether for picture-taking or apple- and carrot-eating, he responds to every attention with heartwarming grunts of delight and swipes of that uncommonly rough tongue just as he always did.

In a country of massive trees and massively violent weather, Bahamas would seem to stand for incredible stamina; for the miracle of survival where death would appear to be nothing less than certain. But those who knew the big Angus best insist that he was indestructible because more than anything he symbolized the enormous power of love. If such be so, this should be fulfillment enough for any living thing.

ACKNOWLEDGMENTS   I wish to express my deepest thanks to the following individuals and agencies for their invaluable help in preparing this story that grew out of the Christmas disaster of 1964 in California's redwood country. All of it greatly supplemented my three and a half decades of experience and knowledge gained through both work and adventure in the giant forests.

Mr. and Mrs. Larry Bush and family, owners of Bahamas.

Mr. and Mrs. George Merriman, neighbors of Bahamas in Klamath Glen.

Mr. and Mrs. Roy Rook, fishing resort owners, Klamath Glen.

Mr. Frank Gehman, Methodist minister, Klamath.

Mr. Courtland Boice, riverboatman and resort owner, Requa.

Numerous residents of Klamath, Klamath Glen, Requa, and Crescent City.

Mr. Dave Stewart, Crescent City, rescuer of Bahamas.

Major Ralph L. Cavalli, Commanding officer, 777th Radar Squadron, Klamath Air Force Station, Requa.

The Crescent City *American*.

Eureka Newspapers, Inc., Eureka.

Mr. Darold G. Richcreek, Harbor Master, Crescent City Harbor District.

Lt. Otto Zigler, Undersheriff, Del Norte County, Crescent City.

Numerous mill owners, loggers, and timber cruisers.

California State Department of Highways.

Mr. Thomas E. Blair, Director of Fairs and Expositions, State Department of Agriculture, Sacramento.

Mr. H. Wallace Moore, Assistant TLO, and Mr. Robert Hale, photographer, U.S. Army Corps of Engineers, San Francisco District.

US. Coast Guard, Samoa.

U.S. Weather Bureau, Eureka.

Mr. A. K. Crebbin, Deputy Forest Supervisor, Klamath National Forest, Yreka.

Mr. W. W. Spinney, Forest Supervisor, Six Rivers National Forest, Eureka.

Mr. Don Hurlbut, Assistant Ranger, Big Bar Ranger District, Shasta-Trinity National Forest, Big Bar, Weaverville.

Mrs. Arlene Whitney, Clerk, Lower Trinity Ranger Station, Salyer, Shasta-Trinity National Forest.

The late Mr. E. P. French, redwood country pioneer, noted timber cruiser, former District Superintendent of District 1 (Redwood Empire), California State Division of Beaches and Parks, Richardson Grove.

Mr. Neal Thomason, Stock Foreman, Cattle Division of Rancho Sespe, breeders of fine Aberdeen Angus, Fillmore.

Mr. and Mrs. Gene Percy, cattle ranchers, Fillmore.

Dr. Charles B. Nelson, veterinarian, Fillmore.

Mr. H. M. ("Buck") Tifft, rancher, Fillmore.

Mrs. Dulcie Arnold, Librarian, Fillmore High School, Fillmore.

Mr. Sterling North, author of *Rascal* and many other books.

Ethel Young, my long-suffering housemate.

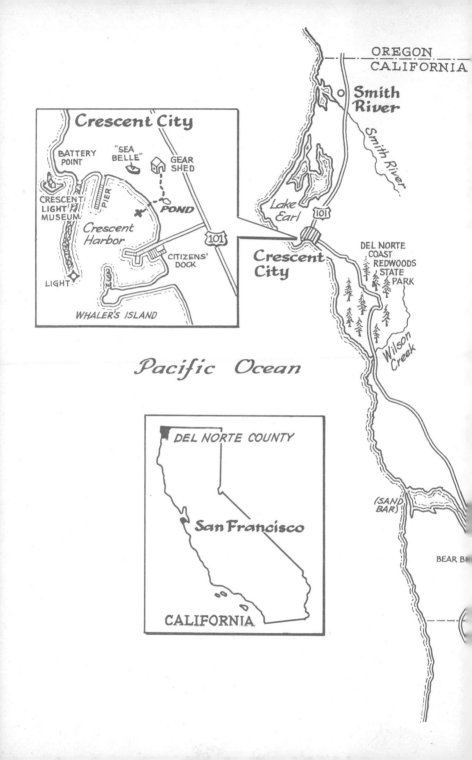